Yesterday's Dreams

YESTERDAY'S DREAMS

ALICE SHARPE

AVALON BOOKS
THOMAS BOUREGY AND COMPANY, INC.
401 LAFAYETTE STREET
NEW YORK, NEW YORK 10003

© Copyright 1991 by Alice Sharpe
Library of Congress Catalog Card Number: 90-93658
ISBN 0-8034-8862-9

PRINTED IN THE UNITED STATES OF AMERICA
ON ACID-FREE PAPER
BY HADDON CRAFTSMEN, SCRANTON, PENNSYLVANIA

For my son, Joseph, who may recognize in Caspar, my cat's appetite and his cat's brain. And for my daughter, Jennifer, whose cat's most memorable habits were tactfully omitted!

Chapter One

I closed the door quietly behind me and tiptoed out into the drawing room. Sunlight streamed through the tall windows, and for one moment, I looked longingly at the pale tapestry sofa positioned so it was bathed in the warm afternoon glow. What I wouldn't give to collapse for a couple of hours and sleep my problems away! But scattered boxes waved cardboard fingers at me, cautioning it wasn't time to quit yet.

Cardboard fingers? I rubbed my eyes; maybe I should take time out for a nap. When inanimate objects began scolding . . . then I noticed that the windows were ajar, allowing the afternoon breeze to blow through the room and flutter the brown packing tape I'd torn loose a few

1

hours earlier. My boyfriend, Danny, had helped me pack; the way he packed suggested he had heavily invested in a tape factory.

A soft meow announced a visitor: Caspar, the friendly cat, ready for a little affection before settling into a snowball shape for his afternoon siesta. I indulged him by perching on the edge of the cushions, but immediately felt uncomfortable. Grandmother's house and furniture might be a good deal more elegant than the hodgepodge of this and that I'd hauled up to my third-story apartment in the heart of downtown Oakland, but it was a good deal more intimidating as well. Caspar leaped gracefully onto my lap, worked his claws a couple of times, and purred his welcome speech.

"I don't have time for this," I told Caspar, who looked at me with yellow-eyed adoration. He was as unlike his mistress, my grandmother, as was possible. Where she was spare and stately, he was a mass of white, long-haired plush; where her attitude was 'Get it done—*now*!', his was 'Let's have a bowl of cat food and a short eight-hour nap first.' I'd once heard Grandmother tell someone that Caspar was the world's most beautiful cat—and the dumbest. She was probably right. On the other hand, look what she thought about me! Maybe I should give Caspar a chance to prove his brainpower on his own.

Caspar abandoned me in favor of the back of the

sofa, where he stretched luxuriously in the sun and began his prenap bath. I watched him for a few seconds; then my gaze drifted to the stern portraits of Grandmother and Grandfather that flanked the small fireplace. Grandfather had died the year before I was born, twenty-five years earlier, so I'd never known him; however, my mother had often assured me he was just as high-minded and discipline-oriented as his portrait suggested. As for Grandmother, twenty years younger than her husband—well, she'd hardly changed since the artist captured her blazing eyes and the defiant tilt of her chin.

My gaze darted to the left. Across the small hall, I could see the closed double doors of Grandmother's music room, and I felt a shiver almost as old as I was tap dance up my spine. For a moment, I thought of marching over and throwing open the doors, but the moment passed and I was still sitting on the sofa. It was amazing that so many years could pass and I could still be so affected by that room and what lay within it.

How was I going to get through the summer in this Victorian museum? How was I supposed to care for a woman who made no bones about the fact that she found me silly and insipid and uninspired, just like my mother? How was I ever going to be able to provide the care she needed without losing myself in the process? And what about Danny? Would he forget all about me in three months and run off with a Las Vegas show girl?

An hour later most of my summer possessions had been hastily stored in the dresser and on the shelves of the bedroom in which I was to spend the summer. Since it was right next to Grandmother's room, I worked as quietly as I could. And since it was her extra room, I had to push her stacks of piano music aside to make room for my things. I put a small framed picture of Danny on the table beside the narrow bed, then sat down on the firm mattress and picked it up.

Danny Gorman—age twenty-six; occupation, soil engineer—stared back at me with his cool green eyes. I'd snapped the photo two months before as we walked in Golden Gate Park, and he'd been a little annoyed. I could almost hear him say, "Not now, Ellie, please. My hair is windblown." He'd been serious about his hair; I'd thought he was joking. The result was a picture of an irritated man in a blue windbreaker, but something about his expression was so familiar, I'd decided to stick it in the frame and bring it to Grandmother's house.

I exchanged the picture for a small box overflowing with paperback books. I'd packed them indiscriminately, just knowing that I was going to need something to do while Grandmother slept. Unfortunately, as I lugged them across the room, the top three layers slid off, thudding onto the floor. I stopped breathing for several seconds, waiting for Grandmother to call out.

"Keep her quiet and well fed," her doctor had directed just that morning. The food part would present no problem, since, despite her trim figure, Grandmother seemed to eat practically anything. But keeping her down was something else. I'd been in Eureka only twelve hours, and already I'd had to threaten to turn on the television if she didn't take a short nap. She hated television, said she kept one around only for the occasional concerts on the public channel. She said everything else was mindless drivel, and maybe she was right. Still, my policy, at least for the summer, was any means to an end. It didn't appear that I'd waked her, however, and I finally resumed breathing.

The doorbell rang as I hung my robe on a hook. I practically killed myself hurdling boxes and half-empty suitcases to get to the door before the bell woke Grandmother.

I made it in the middle of the second ring.

Two men stood on the doorstep, one much younger than the other. My gaze darted between them, but settled on the older and smaller man, because his expression was the more unusual.

His mouth hung open. His eyes popped wide behind his wire-framed glasses. He was wearing a felt hat with a dashing little feather on one side, and as he swallowed—gulped, almost—he took off the hat and held it in trembling hands against his chest.

"Mimi," he whispered.

I shook my head.

"That's not possible," the younger man said, and I shifted my gaze to him.

He was just under six feet tall, with straight brown hair and dark eyes that were currently studying me as though I were a bug under a microscope. He was wearing blue jeans, a T-shirt, and an old leather bomber jacket. The jacket looked authentic, as though it had survived a few World War II bombing raids, and the way the man wore it made it seem possible he'd been along for the ride. Of course, that was impossible as the man inside the coat wasn't a day over thirty.

"I beg your pardon," I said.

"Mimi, don't you recognize me?" This from the older man.

"Granddad . . ." the younger cautioned.

"Have I come in on the middle of something?" I asked.

The old man said, "It's her, Josh. It's my Mimi."

"That's impossible," the younger man repeated, smiling nervously at me, begging me for patience from the depths of his dark eyes.

I turned my attention to the older man. "I'm afraid I'm not your Mimi," I said gently. "My name is Ellen. I don't even live here, not really." They both continued to stare, so I added, "I'm here to take care of my grandmother. She broke her arm." They were both still staring. I added, "Am I getting through to either one of you?"

The younger man shook his head. "It's uncanny," he said. "Show her the picture, Granddad."

The older man took a picture out of the inside pocket of his tweed vest and offered it to me. The fog began to lift as I looked at the picture.

"This is my grandmother," I said, studying a smaller and more worn rendition of the same photograph that sat on the top of my mother's curio cabinet. "This is a picture of Naomi Brookfield, not of me."

"Of course," the younger man said.

The older man poked a crooked finger at the picture. "Same black hair, same blue eyes, same pretty face. You look just like my Mimi."

"But I'm not," I said again. I looked at the younger man for support.

He smiled as he touched his grandfather's arm. "Granddad, this is Naomi's granddaughter, Ellen—"

"Nickleson," I interrupted.

"She just happens to look like Mimi," the young man finished.

As I watched the older man accept the inevitable, I started thinking about this Mimi business. My grandmother was never called by that or any other nickname. In fact, almost everyone outside the family called her

Mrs. Brookfield. Even my father called her Mrs. Brookfield.

"Let me explain," the younger man said. "My name is Josh Holt, and this is my grandfather, Gerald Holt. He used to know your grandmother. Can you imagine how startled he was when you opened the door? You do bear a remarkable likeness to your grandmother, at least when she was your age, don't you?"

I looked at the picture again. I'd heard that kind of talk before, but I'd never seen it myself. Sure, I was sort of tall like Grandmother, and our hair and eye color were the same. I'd just never noticed—or wanted to notice—a family resemblance.

I looked at Gerald Holt and smiled. "You're my grandmother's friend? It must be a while since you've seen her?"

The answer wasn't as fast in coming as it should have been. I mean, it was hardly a trick question. But Gerald stammered a bit, looked uncomfortable, and finally blurted out, "Yes!"

Now that his mouth was closed and his eyes were back in their sockets, he appeared to be an attractive man about Grandmother's age with gentle gray eyes and a whole head of fine white hair. I couldn't help thinking that if he and my grandmother had once been sweethearts, she had chewed him up and spit him out for sport years before.

"I wonder if you might tell her I'm here?" he asked.

"She's had an accident," I told him gently. "Nothing serious, just a broken arm, but the doctor says that at her age, bones don't mend as fast as they used to."

"I could tell you a thing or two about age," Gerald said.

"Well, unfortunately, Grandmother's asleep now. I'll tell her you came by."

Gerald's face fell.

Josh put his arm around his grandfather's shoulders. "We'll come back," he assured him. He looked at me and added, "It's quite important. He's been in Eureka for about six months now, and this is the first time he's gotten the nerve to come even this far."

"I see," I said, though of course I didn't, but the whole thing was beginning to be interesting. "Why don't you come back right after dinner, about seven or so?"

"Yes," Gerald said, putting his hat back on his head as though to finalize the arrangement.

Josh glanced at his watch. "I have that appointment with Brennan at six."

"I could come alone . . ." Gerald began.

Josh smiled. "No, that's okay. It won't take long to show Brennan his boat. If he wants more time, I'll make another appointment for later in the week. Okay, Ellen, we'll be back in a couple of hours."

I closed the door, then parted the curtains and peered through the glass panel. I saw Josh open the passenger door for his grandfather, then walk around to the driver's door of a beat-up old blue Ford pickup, pausing before he climbed in to rub the floppy ears of a huge black Lab who was tied into the bed of the truck. I watched the two men drive away before letting the curtain slip back into place.

Who was this dapper man with the interesting grandson? Obviously, someone from Grandmother's past. The picture he held so dear was taken when Grandmother was in her late teens, when she was about six years younger than I was now, before she and my grandfather had married. Why hadn't Gerald seen my grandmother for over fifty years?

Maybe even more important—from my point of view—was the question of whether he would be willing to help his long-lost "Mimi" fill some of the long summer hours ahead. I most fervently hoped so.

Chapter Two

G randmother was still asleep. I
thought of my friend Jeanie, who
had a baby girl in the apartment above mine. I used
to tease her about how she waited for the baby to wake
up as ardently as she struggled to get her to sleep, until
one day she sighed and said, "Ellen, you just don't
understand. First you work like mad to get them asleep,
then when the nap lasts too long, you begin to worry
that they're getting too much and may never close their
eyes again."

Was Grandmother sleeping too late? Was I going to
spend my summer fussing over her as though she were
seven instead of seventy-five? As if she'd let me.

The house consisted of a middle hall uniting two

11

symmetrical halves. Music room on the left, drawing room on the right, two bedrooms behind the music room, and the study and kitchen beyond the drawing room. The bathroom was located off the kitchen, because when the house had been built a hundred years before, there hadn't been indoor plumbing, so it was tacked on during one of the many renovations.

I wandered through the small house, passing the closed double doors of the music room, purposely avoiding even a glance in their direction. Sooner or later, preferably alone, I was going to have to confront that room. On my third pass by the doors, I finally tore them open.

There it sat, in the same place it had squatted for years, all the way back to when I was a small child and had confronted the thing as an enemy, a crouching three-legged beast with a voice and a mind of its own: Grandmother's black baby-grand piano, waiting, taunting, daring me to touch it, secure with the fact that I'd rather be locked in a Turkish prison for the next twenty years than put one finger on those ivory keys.

Well, this time I would win. This time Grandmother's arm was broken, and not even she would sit here and play this creature, nor would any of her little students, who tortured the thing with their inexperience, unaware it would seek revenge in the form of hours and hours of practice on its comrades.

Okay, I wasn't able to be objective about pianos.

I'd grown up in Eureka, not far from Grandmother, and every Thursday afternoon at four-thirty sharp, I'd been dutifully marched into this room like a lamb to slaughter. My fingers weren't nimble enough. I hadn't practiced properly. I was sloppy and inattentive and I couldn't keep time with the metronome, that wooden pyramid that still sat on Grandmother's piano and which would, even now, with the touch of my hand, begin ticking away, one-two, one-two, with maddening accuracy. In the past, no matter how far I fell behind that infernal machine, would it pause politely, waiting for me to catch up, encouraging me to keep going? No, it just kept ticking, mocking me until beads of perspiration would break out on my forehead and my fingers would fumble again and again.

And behind me, her body towering above my braided hair, stood Grandmother, whispering "one-two, one-two" with the same precision and unrelenting rhythm as the metronome, until things were so hopelessly fouled up that she would finally shriek, "Enough, Ellen! Start again."

Well, not this summer. I wasn't eight years old anymore. I was in charge, not Grandmother. She was supposed to rest, and that meant no piano lessons. I saw her desk in the corner and skirted the edges of the room to search it. I turned on a light, as the room was kept purposely dark for some reason I'd never understood, and immediately saw her appointment book.

Tonight I'd get her to help me make a list of the children whose summers would be spared—though I might phrase it differently to her—and I would call them to cancel lessons for the next three months. Otherwise, tomorrow morning there would be a line of fidgety kids and hopeful parents standing out on the step.

I closed the doors behind me and instantly felt better. Silly, but that's the way it was.

How had I gotten myself into this?

In real life, I was one of three co-owners of a small jewelry store. We specialized in natural items like jade and silver and quartz, and though none of us was getting rich, we were almost always able to pay our bills on time. Yesterday, I'd been happily getting ready for a lazy summer season—afternoons working in the shop, wondering if Danny and I were ever going to get serious about our romance, contemplating whether I should replace the transmission in my car or invest in a newer used model, planning which flowers I'd plant in my window box—when Grandmother fell and I received my mother's subsequent urgent call.

"Ellie, you just have to come nurse your grandmother back to health, honey, you just have to. It's too late for your dad and me to cancel our travel plans, and besides, you know how much we're looking forward to seeing Karen's new baby."

I assured her I knew. I also understood, even though I wished I didn't. She and Father might live in the same city as Grandmother, but contact was minimal. Besides, my parents had arranged to swap houses with a French couple who lived close to my sister Karen's new home in Paris. If they stayed to help Grandmother, they would have to live in her house, as the French couple were in transit when Grandmother hurt herself and would be counting on their Eureka residence for the summer. The thought of my mother and my grandmother coexisting in the same house was bad enough, but my father? No way! They'd tear each other apart.

"Please," Mother had said, setting the hook, pulling me in. Jeanie's younger brother just happened to need a place to stay for the summer, so I was able to sublet him my apartment. My co-owners assured me they could run the store for the summer, that I was not to worry. Danny said he'd miss me but a little time apart might be just what our relationship needed. So, within hours, and more on pity than rational thought, I had assured my mother I could leave that very night. I had packed in a blur, driven north in a blur, arrived seven hours later still in a blur.

Grandmother was not exactly thrilled to see me. "So it's you or a nursing home," she'd remarked when I walked through the door.

Actually, she was dead right.

Grandmother woke up as I was making clam sauce. "Ellen?" she yelled.

I gave Caspar the bite of clam he'd been clamoring for and went to see to Grandmother. She was sitting up in bed, her thin cheeks flushed with sleep, her dark hair slightly mussed.

"Nice nap?" I asked.

"I hate naps," she snapped as I dug around under the bed for her slippers.

"Dinner is almost ready," I said, holding the robe so she could slip her left arm into the sleeve, then draping it over her right arm, which was encased in four inches of plaster and wrapped in a sling.

Caspar jumped up on the bed and rubbed his pretty chin along Grandmother's cast. "What are you cooking?" she asked as she absently rubbed the cat's head.

"Clam sauce. I hope you like it."

"Sometimes. Spaghetti too?"

"Fettuccine. With broccoli."

"That stupid nap gave me a headache. I won't take another nap. Naps are for babies and old geezers, and I am neither."

I nodded. I didn't point out that she'd slept for the better part of three hours. "It's almost ready," I said. "Do you need any more help?"

"I am perfectly capable of going to the bathroom by myself, Ellen. Thank you anyway."

"You're welcome. I'll go stir the sauce, then."

I stirred the sauce, and just when I was thinking of mounting a search-and-rescue mission for Grandmother, she finally emerged from the bathroom. She'd managed to repin her hair into its habitual elegant French twist, apply a touch of red lipstick and a bright spot of rouge on each cheek. In fact, she looked so put together that I wondered what I was doing at her house.

"You didn't make spaghetti because you thought I couldn't manipulate my fork with my left hand, is that right?" she asked.

I spooned dinner onto her plate. Caspar had taken up guard duty under her chair, and he swiped at me with a gloved paw. "I thought it might be hard for you," I admitted. "I was probably wrong."

"I am quite ambidextrous. Comes from mastering the piano."

"I'll remember that," I said.

"This looks good."

"I hope you like it." A summer of this kind of formal conversation was going to drive me batty. I saw Grandmother slip Caspar a piece of clam, but when I looked at her face to exchange bemused smiles, I found her looking the other way.

"What's my appointment book doing on the table?" she asked.

"I thought you and I could go through the names," I told her. "Then tonight I'll call everyone and cancel their lessons for the summer."

Grandmother dropped her fork. It clattered against

her plate and fell onto the floor, still full of noodles and clams. Caspar pounced at once.

"I'll get you a clean fork," I said, standing.

"What do you mean, 'cancel their lessons'?" she gasped.

I set the fork on her plate. She ignored it. "What do you mean?" she demanded.

"I thought it would be impossible for you to play the piano with a broken arm."

"Of course I can't play the piano with a broken arm, but I can still teach."

"Dr. Pullman said—"

"Phooey! What does he know about art? He listens to something called 'easy rock,' whatever that is supposed to mean. Elevator music. You can't listen to a man like that."

"Well, maybe not about music, but about medicine—"

"I *will* teach my classes, young lady, make no mistake. There is a recital on the first Sunday in August— there is a recital on the first Sunday of *every* August— my students will not miss it."

I capitulated at once, sensing that the argument was not only futile but also worse for her health and peace of mind than fatigue. Besides, a few days of lessons might go further toward convincing her that it was better to take the summer off than a thousand words uttered by me. "Okay. But promise me you'll talk to Dr. Pullman about it."

"I promise," she said. She didn't mean it. I knew she didn't mean it. Furthermore, I had the sneaking suspicion that she knew I knew she didn't mean it. We called a truce.

"How is Mrs. Hollis next door?" I asked, more to have a conversation than because of any real fondness for Mrs. Hollis. Quite the contrary. She'd been crabby when I was a kid, scolding me for things I didn't do, complaining to my grandmother that I was being raised poorly. No doubt my grandmother totally agreed.

"She's dead and gone," Grandmother said.

I coughed. "That's too bad."

"You never liked her, and she never liked you."

I decided to steer this in a different direction. "Well, that means you have different neighbors. Have you met them? Are they nice?"

She shrugged. "Ellen, I don't have time to make friends with my neighbors, especially when they're no older than you."

"Oh." End of that topic. "Have another noodle," I told Caspar as I hand-fed him a tiny morsel. By the end of the summer, it was a good bet Caspar and I were going to be close friends.

"We do not feed the cat from the table," Grandmother said.

I laughed, thinking she was actually making a joke.

"But you gave him a bite a second ago," I protested when she regarded me with impassive eyes.

"You are mistaken. You'll find, Ellen, that I keep an organized house. Caspar is a cat. He doesn't get on the furniture, and he doesn't eat people food, especially not from the table."

I knew I was staring at her with a stupid expression on my face, but I couldn't help it. Was she serious? Was this her way of teasing me or something? She continued eating her dinner in silence. If this was a joke, it was the best-kept joke in town.

The doorbell rang, startling me. It wasn't until that second that I remembered Gerald and Josh Holt.

"I have a surprise for you," I said, standing abruptly.

"You'd better get the door first," Grandmother said as she allowed Caspar to jump onto her lap.

"That's the surprise." I stood there, mesmerized by the sight of Caspar licking my grandmother's hand with his little pink tongue. She made no effort to stop him. She didn't even seem to notice he was doing it.

"What's the surprise?" she prompted.

"What? Oh, you had a visitor from your past today, a Mr. Gerald Holt. He came while you were asleep—"

I stopped talking because Grandmother's face had literally drained of color. I'd never seen that happen before, but it was as though someone had dipped her face in liquid chalk, and all that showed now were her bright blue eyes and the two small circles of red rouge on her cheeks. I saw her hand shake as it rested on Caspar's back. "Who?" she croaked.

The doorbell rang again.

"Gerald Holt. He seems to be your age, maybe a few years older. He's a nice-looking man with white hair—Well, it wouldn't have been white years ago, would it?" I realized I was babbling and finished lamely, "He called you his Mimi."

"Gerry," she whispered, her voice suddenly vulnerable.

The doorbell rang again, and I moved to answer it.

"Wait!" The desperate urgency in Grandmother's voice even got through to Caspar, who twitched his ears.

I waited. Finally, as the bell rang yet again, she said, "Don't answer it."

"I have to, Grandmother. I told them to come at seven. Don't you want—"

She stood up, sending the cat flying across the floor. "Get rid of him, then. I won't see him. I won't!" She hurried toward her bedroom, and I heard the door slam as the bell rang one last time.

Chapter Three

 " " She's just too tired for company," I lied.

"But you said she took a nap this afternoon," Gerald reminded me.

I swallowed. "Yes, that's true, but it was . . . it was restless. You know how that can happen when you're sick and everything? You just get to sleep, and then you roll over and it hurts. . . ."

Josh regarded me with narrowed, suspicious eyes.

Gerald said, "Please, Miss Nickleson. I must see her."

"I'm sorry," I said. "I really am. Maybe you could check back, by phone, in a few weeks. I don't know."

Gerald Holt had his hat clamped against his chest

23

again. The evening had turned chilly, as evenings often did in northern California coastal towns, even in the summer, and Gerald had added a thin black coat to his ensemble. His grandson was still in his bomber jacket.

"I see," Gerald said, and I got the feeling that he really did see, that whatever strange reasons my grandmother might have for not meeting with him were understood. Josh apparently didn't get quite the same feeling.

"Won't see us, Ellen, or are you taking the job of nursemaid a little too seriously?"

"Josh," Gerald admonished wearily.

"I resent that statement," I said, fuming.

"Well, I resent my grandfather's being denied access to this woman because her officious granddaughter wants to play nurse."

Speechless, I just stared at him.

Gerald said, "Josh, son, just shut up. You don't know what you're talking about."

"Well, maybe I would if you weren't so . . . so mysterious about everything. You looked up this woman's name five-and-a-half months ago, Granddad. Don't bother denying it, I saw you. And then you started singing that old song 'Gigi,' only you substituted Mimi for Gigi. And then this afternoon when I finally get you to come over here, what do we do? Sit in the truck for forty-five minutes while you work up the courage to ring the doorbell, that's what we do. Then the woman is napping, so we motor back to the island, then back here, and now this little—''

"Watch it!" I warned. As he indulged himself in this tirade, I began to understand that he wasn't really mad at me, just super-frustrated with his grandfather. Maybe he didn't even know it yet, and ranting and raving against me was preferable to facing what was really bothering him.

I addressed myself to Gerald. "I'm sorry. My grandmother slipped on the steps around back the day before yesterday. She broke her right arm, and she's still weak and tired. Please, just go away tonight and call before coming again. I'm really very, very sorry."

Josh stalked off down the sidewalk. Gerald nodded at me, whispered thanks, and followed his hotheaded grandson.

I closed the door.

"You shouldn't have apologized to him," Grandmother said from the shadows. She'd been in the front drawing room the whole time, lurking behind the cherry-wood secretary.

She moved into the light. At seventy-five, she was still striking, with her dark hair (courtesy of Miss Clairol), her high cheekbones, her tall figure wrapped in red velour. Only the big white cast looked out of place, like a plaster alien stuck to her side.

"Why didn't you tell him yourself, then?" I asked.

"I won't talk to that man."

"But you heard him. You saw—"

"I saw nothing. I only heard his voice. That was enough."

"Why?"

"I won't talk about him, either," she said imperiously.

We stared at each other, neither of us giving ground.

Finally, I sighed, admitting a stalemate. "If you're going to teach your classes tomorrow, then I suppose we'd better alter your clothes so the arms will fit over that cast," I said.

"Good thinking," my grandmother agreed.

"One-two, one-two."

I heard it in my sleep, and now I heard it as I chopped vegetables for soup. Inside the music room, a little boy of about nine years of age was trying desperately to get through a song I could barely recognize. My heart went out to him.

"That's enough!" Grandmother cried. After a lengthy pause she said, her voice under control again, "Now one more time. Start over at the beginning, Stewart. And this time, remember, staccato!"

Stewart began again. It was no better than the time before, and for the first time, I felt a stab of sympathy for my grandmother, who had to listen to all this sense-less pounding of her beloved piano keys and pretend she found enough musical promise to justify future lessons.

Caspar jumped up on the drainboard and looked at the carrots and onions with an aggrieved eye. "No meat up here, buddy," I told him, nudging him down with my elbow.

I'd spent half the night wondering about Gerald Holt and my grandmother and what had happened between them fifty-five years in the past. Had he really called her Mimi? I couldn't even imagine her accepting that, couldn't picture her doe-eyed and loving, couldn't hear her giggling softly in his arms. He must have worshiped her from afar, and she must have swatted him down with the same concern with which she'd rid her life of a housefly.

The other half of the night, or so it seemed, I'd spent wondering about Josh Holt, wishing I knew if he was still angry at me, which just made me mad at myself because if there was an innocent victim in this mess, it was me. It wasn't my fault my grandmother wouldn't talk to his grandfather. She'd probably jilted him five-and-a-half decades ago, and it looked as if she was going to do it again.

The phone rang as I put the vegetables in with the stock. I answered it on the sixth ring, after Grandmother yelled at me to stop what I was doing and take care of the phone. It looked as though I was not only chief cook and bottle washer, maid and driver, cat companion and laundress, but also telephone operator/message taker. In fact, how did this woman manage when she had to handle all these chores alone?

"Is that you, Ellen?"

"Danny?"

"Of course."

I suddenly realized how much I missed everything at home. I missed the creaking pipes in my apartment, the smog outside the window, the sirens late at night, the street people, the beggars, the vagrants. "I miss you a lot," I said.

"Me too," he said, as though missing me were a novel and surprising discovery. "I went by the store this morning," he added. "Susie wants me to tell you that a whole shipment of quartz crystals came in first thing. You'd special-ordered a smoky topaz for some lady from Santa Clara or something?"

"Lila Keene, that's right."

"Well, Susie wants to know if she should call this Lila and tell her it's in."

"It's a smoky topaz with a blue topaz set on the fourteen-karat gold finding. Yes, she should call Lila."

"I'll be seeing Susie this evening, so I'll pass along the message."

"Okay. Why will you be seeing Susie this evening?"

A long pause. "Well, you might as well know. I got the Halverson job, you know, the junior-college extension. I'll be in charge of the foundation."

"That's great, Danny. Congratulations!"

"Thanks. Anyway, the boss is throwing a big party, and I can't show up stag."

"So you asked Susie?"

"You don't have any objections, do you?"

"Of course not," I said, not sure if that was the truth.

"I mean, you're three hundred and fifty miles north of here."

"I know."

"Good. Well, now, you just relax and enjoy your summer, Ellen. It'll do you good to get away for a while."

"It's like being on a cruise ship up here," I said. "All fun and games, no work. Grandmother is a darling, and all I do all day long is sit around and eat bonbons."

"See? I told you you'd have fun."

"I'm being sarcastic, Danny."

"Whatever. What's all that racket in the background?"

"That's Stewart trying to plow his way through

something I believe is called 'Eskimo Boy.' I could be wrong; it's kind of hard to tell."

Another long pause. "Well, you take care, Ellen. See you in a couple of months."

"Wait!" I realized he was ready to hang up and I was going to lose my only link to the outside world. "Wait a second. Danny, do you think you might get free for a weekend? You could drive up here. It's really beautiful. I could show you where I was born, and we could go to the beach—"

"It's a long drive," he said.

"Just six hours."

"And I've got the Halverson job now, you know. We'll see."

"Right," I said.

"Good-bye, Ellen."

"Good-bye, Danny."

"You take care," he added before he hung up, and I replaced the receiver feeling more than a little confused.

"Stewart!" Grandmother snapped, her voice carrying through the house like a pistol shot. One last inharmonious chord, then blessed silence.

"Begin again," Grandmother said. I could just imagine the agony in Stewart's mind as the hands on the clock slowed down and crept around the face, conspiring with the piano to keep him in torture as long as possible. When I heard the front doorbell and realized it must be his mother to pick him up, I felt just as much relief as he must have felt.

"Ellen?" Grandmother barked. "Get the door!"

"My after-lunch lesson is more advanced," Grandmother told me over lunch.

I ached to help her get the broth to her mouth. It seemed every time she got the spoon close with her left hand, it twisted and most of the contents dribbled back into the bowl. I got up, took a couple of mugs from the cupboard, and dumped the contents of our bowls into them.

"What did you do that for?" she asked.

Wasn't it obvious? There was no answer that she'd accept, so I just shrugged and repeated her last statement, "Your afternoon lesson is more advanced?"

"That's right. This soup is delicious. I'm going to get fat this summer."

"You could use a few pounds."

"So could you. I won't need you this afternoon, you know. I think you should get out of this house for a while. Take a walk. Go to a movie. I know how fond you are of video distractions."

I laughed softly. "The walk sounds great. I'll tour the old hometown on foot."

"That's fine."

"If you're sure you won't need me here—"

"I realize I would be rotting away in a nursing home if your mother hadn't convinced you to take time out of your busy life to come here and nursemaid me," she said. "Not that I need the nursing, but she and Dr. Pullman were convinced I needed someone at the house." She put the mug down and added, "If I had the money, I wouldn't take music students."

It was just enough of a non sequitur to make me look up. "Huh?"

"I wouldn't take music students if I didn't need the money to buy my food. I would concentrate on my own work."

"I see," I said. I didn't.

"And I wouldn't keep you hostage up here if I could afford to hire a maid."

Ah, the light dawned. I said carefully, "I'm thrilled you need me, Grandmother."

"Naturally. You're like your mother, content to be needed by other people. I'm a strong woman, Ellen. Perhaps a little of my self-reliance will rub off on you this summer."

I swallowed every nasty word I felt like hurling at her. She was old and probably in pain, and this was her house. I didn't know how many times I could stuff resentment and anger down my own throat, but I managed this time with no more than a nervous tic in my eye.

"I'm going for a walk," I said, rising. "Just leave the dishes on the table. I'll clean up later." I almost tripped on Caspar as I made my way to the door and freedom.

Chapter Four

Grandmother lived in an old part of town where the sidewalks were wide, the houses old-fashioned, and the children plentiful. It was a beautiful summer afternoon, and the relief I felt at being free of the house, the piano, and my tyrannical grandmother was so tangible I could taste it.

I wandered down toward the waterfront, pausing every now and then to gaze into shop windows. It was the first day of summer vacation, and children hassled their mothers for ice cream, their voices loud and insistent, their laughter infectious. All I needed, I mused as I walked, was Danny's hand in mine.

Wait. Danny didn't like children. He said they took

time away from a couple and that marriages were stronger if there were no children involved. I suspected his views on this subject might change with time; on the other hand, maybe they wouldn't. Was I in love with Danny Gorman? And if I was, did I love him enough to risk something like this, because I kind of liked the idea of being a mom someday. The whole thing might be academic, anyway, I reminded myself. Danny had spent twenty-four hours alone before contacting Susie, one of my co-owners. And here I'd been worrying about show girls!

I stopped walking when I got to Humboldt Bay and could go no farther. The tide was in, so I walked down a gently sloping ramp to stand on what appeared to be a new dock. It was only about six feet wide and maybe twelve feet long, and there were two big cleats for tying up boats. Between the cleats was an open skiff with a small red motor, lines leading fore and aft and wrapping around the cleats. The boat was empty except for a pair of old oars.

I sat down cross-legged on the dock. A sailboat passed on its way back to the marina that was located on a small island across from me, and the skipper, a young woman with red hair and a bright yellow coat, waved merrily. I returned her wave. I scooted closer to the edge of the dock on the end away from the skiff, and dipped my hand into the cold salty water. Long thin strands of eel grass waved in the murky depths, or so it seemed. The water at the shore like this couldn't have been more than five or six feet deep.

I admired the boats in the marina for a while; then I closed my eyes against the glare from the water, content for the time being to feel the sun on my face and the wind ruffle my hair. I tried to empty my mind and not think about Danny and—especially—not think about Grandmother, but her parting words at the house had sunk in deeper than I thought.

Was I just a simple-minded people pleaser? Was my mother? And if we were, was that so bad?

"Mimi?"

A man's voice jerked me out of my musing.

"I mean Ellen," he said contritely. Gerald Holt stood on the dock, a paper grocery bag in his arms. I could see that finding me there had yanked him into the past again. "I thought for a moment . . ." he said, shaking his head. "What you must think of me!"

"Is this your dock?" I asked as I stood.

"It's Josh's dock." His eyes brightened as he asked, "Has your grandmother changed her mind about seeing me? Is that why you came down here?"

I was glad I could drop the pretense Grandmother was too ill to see him. "She hasn't changed her mind," I said, hating the disappointment I could see flooding his eyes.

"Then why did you come?"

"I came by accident. I was out taking a walk, and this dock was empty and so clean and inviting. . . . I had no idea it was yours."

He said, "Oh."

Boy, did I want to ask him what had happened between him and Grandmother!

"Would you take her a note?" he asked. "A note from me?"

I will not talk to that man, she'd said. "I don't know what good it will do," I told him truthfully.

"It'll make me feel better." Gerald put the sack down on the dock and patted his pockets. "I don't have a pencil or a pen. Do you?"

I'd left the house without a purse. I shook my head. "I'm sorry."

"Will you come out to the island with me?" he asked.

I looked across the bay, past Woodley Island, the one with the marina, toward Oyster Island beyond it. "You live over there?"

"I live with Josh. See, that's his house, right over there." He pointed to a small white house with a larger building beside it. "He lives on Oyster Island. Please, Ellen, I know I'm asking a lot, but do you think you could possibly come across with me? I'd bring you right back. It wouldn't take more than half an hour or so."

I glanced at my watch. If I played my cards right,

I'd miss all the afternoon piano lessons. "I'd love to," I said.

So he stuck the bag of groceries in the boat, back in the stern with him, positioned me on the middle seat, untied the stern line while I untied the bow, started the outboard engine, and we began our journey across the bay.

I loved boats, and today, with the sky above blue and clear, with pelicans making their comical dives for fish, with gulls squawking and fishing boats chugging out to the mouth of the bay to cross over the bar to the ocean, it was better than ever.

It took only ten minutes to reach another dock, this one adjacent to Oyster Island. Tied up to the float were two boats. One was a twenty-five-foot sailboat with sleek lines and new paint, and the other was a functional-looking motorboat with an enclosed cabin. Gerald headed for the clear spot in the middle.

Off to the right of the dock, I saw what appeared to be railroad tracks leading out of the water into a big wooden garage. Beside the garage was a small single-story house painted white with pine-green trim, and behind the house, on a forty-foot-high framework, was what appeared to be a wooden water tank.

A big black Lab with a smiling face and a lolling pink tongue raced down the long wharf and scrambled across the floating dock. Gerald killed the engine, and we drifted toward the dock, the tide helping us along.

The dog was perched on the edge of the float. "Get back, Quincy, you fool dog," Gerald said.

Quincy jumped into the boat. I'm afraid I squealed, sure the boat was going to overturn. Gerald yelled at the dog, who apparently got the message, because he immediately jumped back onto the dock again. Gerald said, "Sit!" and Quincy meekly sank to his stomach.

"Darn animal does that every time," Gerald said. "Grab the dock line, will you?"

I did as directed. We tied up the boat and got out, me handing the grocery sack to Gerald. Quincy was on his feet by now, and I was getting a canine once-over. Maybe he smelled Caspar, because the legs of my jeans at about cat height were getting a particularly close inspection.

"Give it a rest!" Gerald said fondly. Quincy backed away and started jumping around. I saw why when Gerald threw the dog a small piece of candy.

"It must be wonderful living over here," I said as we climbed a ramp up to the dock.

Gerald nodded. "It belonged to my oldest son, Josh's Uncle Wesley. He died a few years ago when a drunken driver swerved up on a sidewalk and ran him down."

"I'm sorry—"

He waved away my sympathy. "Josh has the place now. He's a dedicated boat builder, just like his uncle. Come inside while I write my note," he added as we neared the end of the wharf. The length was necessary because of the tidal influences that changed the level of the water by eight to ten feet every six hours.

It occurred to me that Josh might be in the house. The last thing I wanted to do was to face him again. "I'll wait outside for you," I said.

"I won't be a minute. Look around, make yourself at home." He veered off toward the house, Quincy hot on his heels, and I wandered about.

The place had been a boat yard when I was a kid. I could remember my dad telling me that that was where fishing boats were hauled out prior to fishing season. I also remembered my dad pointing out Wesley Holt in a store one day, and the impression that still remained with me was of a tall man with a ready smile, a curl of pipe smoke circling his head. My father had spoken a few words to the man while I watched, bored. Dad had written me while I was off at college. He'd told me about the boat owner's sudden death in a stupid car accident, and since my dad was an attorney, he'd also said he was representing the man's heirs in a wrongful-death suit.

The ground was alternately muddy sand and fragments of white shells. Scattered here and there were rusty old oil drums, ship parts, fraying ropes, crab pots and faded floats, pieces of weathered lumber, big stainless-steel tanks that probably held water or propane for cooking and heat. The constant sound of a generator came from a shed out back. It was all very picturesque.

I walked toward the open doors of the long garage. I could see a boat hull inside, and, curious, I walked toward it. The garage was huge, probably thirty feet high and fifty or more feet long. Smack in the middle ran the same train tracks as outside. It was obviously part of a system designed for moving boats in and out of the water. Along the walls were workbenches covered with tools, and the salty air smelled of freshly sawed wood.

The hull was that of a sailboat, about thirty feet long, with a round bottom and a centerboard keel, graceful even in its wooden cradle, even on dry land. It appeared work had proceeded to the inside, because except for bottom paint, the mast, and rigging, the outside looked complete.

I tripped on an electrical cord, and I saw the light inside the cabin waver.

"About time you got back! Is lunch ready? I'm starving!"

Josh Holt. I almost made it out of the garage before his voice stopped me: "So, it's you again."

I turned slowly. He was up on the deck of the boat, a good ten feet above me, hands on his waist, a thoughtful scowl on his face.

"Yes, it's me again."

"Stay there," he ordered, and like the meek little sap my grandmother thought I was, I stayed there while he climbed down a ladder propped against the stern. I got a better look at him as he walked toward me, slapping his hands together to clean off the wood dust. He was wearing baggy jeans and a tan T-shirt that conformed to his muscles. He hadn't shaved that morning, so his jaw was dark with stubble. His eyes pinned me to the spot, his gaze unwavering, his mouth a hard line to read. He was a very good-looking man, a fact that, at that moment, I was unable to appreciate.

"I'm glad you're here," he said.

"What?"

"I'm glad you're here," he repeated, this time louder, as though I were a little deaf.

"I can hear you," I said. "I'm just surprised. I didn't think you'd like finding me at your house."

"I wanted to talk to you."

"Well, here I am."

"Yes." He looked down at his feet, and then back at my face, hitching his hands on his waist, biting at the corner of his bottom lip. "I owe you an apology. A profuse, sincere, earnest apology."

Well, well, well, I thought.

"I mean it," he said. "I had no right blaming you for the way things were last night. There's no excuse except . . . well, if you understood . . . not that I do, mind you, but if you did, I'm sure it would all make sense.'' He looked as confused by what he'd just said as I was, which immediately warmed my heart toward him.

"I accept your apology. To tell you the truth, it's occurred to me that you weren't really angry, just frustrated.''

"Yes.'' He stared down at me. I had no idea what he was thinking; I was getting around to appreciating his natural good looks. He was so unlike Danny, not just in coloring, but in disposition and bearing. I felt more comfortable with Danny than I did with this man, but even if a magic genie were to pop out of one of the paint cans lined up against the wall and offer to switch the two men, I knew I wouldn't even consider it. That realization was a tad disconcerting.

He cleared his throat. "How did you get here?''

"Gerald brought me. He found me loitering on your town-side dock and asked me to come over so he could send a note home with me to give to my grandmother.''

"Hope seems to spring eternal,'' Josh observed.

I gestured to the boat behind him and asked, "Did you really build this yourself?''

He turned slightly, treating me to a good look at his profile: strong jaw, nice nose, great eyebrows.

"She's one of Uncle Wes's designs, twenty-nine feet long. I'm building her for a lawyer here in town.''

"Oh? Which one?''

"Doug Brennan. Do you know him?''

"I've heard my father mention the name," I said.

Josh looked down at me. "So, you are related to Mike Nickleson?"

"He's my father."

"And your grandmother—"

"Is my mother's mother, though no two women on the face of the earth have less in common."

"I owe your father a lot," Josh said softly. "He represented me in court after my uncle's . . . accident."

"I know," I said.

"It was kind of a . . . vindication, I suppose," he added. "Uncle Wes always hiked around town, but the insurance company tried to make it sound as though he was partially responsible for that kid's running him down, as though he'd been at the party forcing drinks down the kid's throat, as though Uncle Wes had no right to be walking down the middle of a sidewalk after ten o'clock."

"My father admired your uncle," I said.

Josh nodded. "Have you had lunch? Will you join us?"

I was about to say I'd already eaten when two things occurred to me, not necessarily in this order. One: If Gerald was the cook and he had to run me back to Eureka, then come back here himself, then Josh's lunch was a good forty-five minutes away and anyone could tell he was hungry. Two: Grandmother would still be teaching piano, and the house would still be jumping off its cracked foundation.

"I'd love something to eat," I said.

He smiled slowly. "Good."

The three of us ate slices of avocado on cream-cheese-smeared crackers, outside, on a weather-beaten old picnic table that was probably older than I was. On the ground around the table were different boat parts, from rusty engines to a silver rowboat, weeds gushing harmlessly through the caved-in side. Huge cypress trees provided a windbreak, and snowy white egrets nestled in the top branches like Christmas decorations in June. The sandy ground was littered with clam shells, broken and bleached, pleasantly crunchy underfoot.

Quincy sat by Josh's leg, begging cream cheese. Grandmother might say she didn't feed her cat from the table, but Josh practiced it. "Get away, you miserable mutt," he said affectionately, and Quincy sat down, his chin resting on Josh's knee as if by old habit.

Gerald ate nothing. Several times, I caught him studying me when he thought I wasn't looking. I wondered who and what he saw, and wished there was something I could do to ease the pain in his eyes.

"Do I really look so much like my grandmother?" I asked him as Josh and I began clearing the table.

"I'm sorry," he said. "I know I've been staring at

you. It's just that yes, you do look very like her. You move the way she moved, and your eyes sparkle with the same joy.''

I sank down onto the old bench. "Joy?"

He shrugged self-consciously. I noticed Josh had stopped petting Quincy and was listening too.

"I met her when she was just eighteen," he said. "I was twenty. My father was a dairy farmer; her father had run the mercantile until the year before, when he died in a flu epidemic. That's when her mother began giving piano lessons to make ends meet. I . . . I met Mimi when I went to her house to collect my brother's daughter after her lesson. Mimi answered the door.

"You should have seen her! She was wearing a pink-colored dress. There was a little bit of lace up around the top of the collar. When she breathed, the lace would flutter . . . I thought she was the most bewitching creature I'd ever seen.''

Grandmother! I could imagine her bewitching—she was still very attractive—but in pink and lace!

"What happened?" Josh asked gently.

"She. . . ." He shook his head, snapping out of the past, his eyes refocusing as he stood. "I'll get you the note and a little something else that may persuade her to change her mind," he said curtly.

So it was over. Josh and I walked toward the dock. We didn't say anything as we walked. As we stood looking out across the bay toward the city, I wondered when and if our paths would cross again.

''I'll take you back,'' he said suddenly.

''Okay.''

''I'll tell Granddad. Wait here.'' He ran back toward the house, and I felt a smile spring to my lips.

Chapter Five

"I need to buy wood glue anyway," Josh said as we buzzed back across the bay.

"Of course," I said, mentally chastising myself. What had I thought, that he was as reluctant for our afternoon to end as I was? I saw Danny's face in the waves, laughing with me.

We tied the boat up and lingered a moment on the dock. "What did Granddad give you with the note?" he asked.

"I'm not sure," I said.

We both studied the short piece of faded purple ribbon tied around a tiny model of a piano, gold flecks of paint still clinging tenaciously to the wood. When

Gerald had handed it to me, he'd said, "Give her this too. Ask her if she remembers."

I'd been dying to blurt out, "Are you absolutely, positively one hundred percent sure you have the right woman? Are you really thinking of Naomi Brookfield?" I didn't, of course, but I couldn't seem to merge his image of Grandmother as a soft and sentimental romantic heroine with mine of a sharp-tongued tyrant. How could this man purposely want to be hurt by the same woman twice in a lifetime?

"I wish I knew what had happened between those two," Josh said, his thoughts apparently paralleling my own.

"He won't tell you?"

"Not a word." He sighed deeply, pushing his hands into his jacket pockets, his eyes dark as they scanned my face. "And your grandmother?"

"Refuses to talk about him."

"Will she budge?"

I shook my head. "No."

"I don't know what I'm going to do. He's not eating, and I don't think he's sleeping, either. I hear him pacing in the middle of the night, though he swears it isn't him, blames it on Quincy. He seems kind of distant lately too. He's the last relative I have, so there's no one else to enlighten me."

"I know. My mother might know something, but she's on her way to France. Well, Grandmother will probably reject this note too, so maybe your grand-father will have to accept it and get on with his life.''

"Yeah," Josh said uncertainly. "Do you want a ride? I rent a garage to park the truck in, for when it rains or I need to haul things around."

"No, thanks, I'd rather walk," I told him.

"Me too."

We began walking toward town. I hadn't worn a watch, so I had no idea what time it was, and, truth be known, I didn't want to know. This whole thing was coming to an end of its own accord; soon enough I'd be back in Grandmother's kitchen cooking her meals, helping her with her slippers, driving her to doctor appointments. Meanwhile, it was nice to walk with Josh, the sun making long shadows, the air brisk and tangy with salt.

I paused by a jewelry store with a HELP WANTED sign in the window, and Josh looked at the display with me. "Nice stuff," he said.

"It's jade."

"Even those purple things?" he asked, pointing at a string of beads.

"Yep. As a matter of fact, it's called plum jade. In our shop, we have some that we get from the Su-Chou province of China. Actually, it's just colored jade, but they do a marvelous job."

"And what's that?" he asked, pointing at a deep-blue abalonelike pendant.

"Paua shell from New Zealand. Maori chieftains used to wear it. It's pretty, isn't it?"

I looked up when he didn't answer, and he smiled shyly at me. "I was just thinking it's the same color as your eyes."

I had the horrible feeling my cheeks burst into flames—it sure felt as though they did. I looked back at the paua shell, but my gaze rested this time on our reflections in the glass.

He was a head taller than I and though my hair was longer and darker, he had a tan from all the running back and forth across the bay. I saw a flash of white teeth and knew he was aware of what I was looking at.

"You own a shop like this one?" he asked.

"More or less. I own it with two other women, sisters named Susie and Melissa North. It's down in Oakland."

"So you're from the bay area?"

"Originally from Eureka, but I've been gone eight years. I hardly know anyone here anymore."

We resumed walking. Once in a while his hand brushed mine, and I pretended I didn't notice. All in all, I was sorry when it was time for our paths to part. Who knew when and if we'd ever meet again, and he was sure better company than my crotchety grandmother.

"Grandmother's house is this way," I said, motioning east.

"I know, and the hardware store is this way. Ellen, it's been a fun day. I've . . . enjoyed myself."

"Thanks for lunch," I said. "I've enjoyed myself too."

"Maybe we can do it again sometime. You're here for the summer?"

"It looks like it, yes. And I'd like that."

He smiled warmly. "Good." Then he was gone. I watched his confident stride retreating down the sidewalk for quite a while.

"Where in the world were you?" Grandmother snapped as I closed the front door. She was in the front hall, her good hand pinned to her waist.

"I was out," I said, stating the obvious.

"For four hours? Where?"

"I was gone for four hours, really?"

She narrowed her eyes, and I'm afraid it crossed my mind to take the chicken's way out and lie to her, tell her I'd been rotting away in a dark theater, confirm her worst suspicions. Then I remembered I couldn't lie now—I'd get caught later when I gave her Gerald's note and the miniature piano.

"I'm hungry," she said.

I stopped worrying about myself and looked at her more closely. "Have you been taking the pain medicine

Dr. Pullman left for you?'' I asked. ''You look kind of washed-out.''

She shrugged her good shoulder. ''I don't know where it is.''

''It's in the kitchen on the windowsill where you told me to put it.''

''I can't be a proper teacher when I'm all doped up.''

''That's why you probably shouldn't be teaching. Are you ready to at least cut back on the lessons?''

That was enough. The moment of helplessness vanished in one blink of her blue eyes. ''I will not!''

''Okay. But at least take a pill now, and I'll make you something to eat.''

''I want spaghetti,'' she said, and preceded me into the kitchen.

After dinner, we sat in front of a fire that wasn't needed. Grandmother read a book, Caspar lounged on the back of her chair, and I ripped the underarm seam out of the right sleeve of another one of her blouses. The clock in the hall ticked away the minutes as I struggled to come up with the right words, the right intonation, the right *something* that would convince Grandmother just to read Gerald's note. My mind was a blank, though.

I finally cleared my throat and put aside the sewing. ''This is for you,'' I said and handed her Gerald's note.

She studied me a moment before taking it. "What is this?" she asked as she unfolded the paper. She looked at it for no more than ten seconds, then she stood abruptly as though she were a puppet and the puppeteer had yanked her strings.

"Where did you get this?" she demanded.

"I ran into Gerald Holt today, and he begged me to bring you a message. Just read it, Grandmother."

She wadded the paper and threw it into the flames. "I will not read anything that man has to say."

Belatedly, I remembered the little piano, and took it from my pocket. "He asked me to give this to you too," I said. "He asked me to ask you if you remember. What's he talking about, Grandmother?"

As she looked at the faded ribbon and the delicate trinket, I thought I saw several emotions race across her face. First, tenderness, quickly overtaken by sadness, even more quickly crystallizing into anger. Gradually, a cold mask slipped into place over her features. "I do not remember anything about that man," she said, obviously lying through her teeth.

"But, Grandmother. Maybe if you talked to him, or at least talked to me—"

"Ellen, I do not need your sympathy or your concern. I disposed of that thing once by mailing it away. You get rid of it this time. And in the future, I would appreciate it if you would remember where your loyalties are and do everything in your power not to associate with . . . him. I would expect at least that much from you.'' She nodded her head as though dotting an exclamation point, and stalked out of the room.

I looked at the pitiful scrap of ribbon and the little piano. If they could only talk! I started to throw them both into the fire, but at the last moment, I put them back into my pocket. What was I going to tell Gerald?

''We'll have to tell him the truth,'' Josh said.

It was the next afternoon, and though Grandmother had cast a suspicious eye when I announced an after-lunch walk, she'd not said a word about Gerald Holt. She had reminded me to be back early, as she needed me to drive her to her doctor's appointment, then she'd welcomed a young student who had played the first movement of Beethoven's *Moonlight* Sonata (poorly) four times before I rinsed the last dish and escaped out the back door.

''I should have just told him on the phone,'' I said, shivering in the cool wind that had risen since the fog burned off that morning. The bay wasn't a calm pond like the day before; it was wind-tossed liquid indigo even though the sky was clear and brilliant. Josh's jacket was covered with dark wet spots where it had been splashed as he motored across the bay. We stood on his dock, which was gently jerking beneath us as the tiny waves broke against the rocks.

''No, I'm glad you agreed to meet me here and tell

me about it. I would rather break the bad news to him myself."

"Anyway, now he'll have to accept the fact that Grandmother isn't going to see him or talk to him. He can put this behind him and get on with things."

Josh shrugged as though he knew it wasn't going to be that easy. "You're shivering," he said as he took off his jacket.

"No, no, I'm fine."

"You're shaking like a leaf," he insisted as he held the jacket open for me.

"I left in a hurry," I admitted as I put my arms into the warm jacket. I took Gerald's keepsakes from my jeans pocket and handed it to Josh. "Give them back to him. She wouldn't even touch them."

Josh took them and turned them over and over in his hands. I noticed today that they were woodworker's hands: lightly callused, strong, capable hands. "What do you think?" he asked at last. "Were they in love once?"

I nodded. "I think so. I can't imagine all this suffering over a failed business venture. And then there's this little piano. It seems personal."

"Tell me about her," he said.

I shrugged. "I can't, not really."

"But she's your grandmother."

I kicked a broken mussel shell that a sea gull had left on the dock; it fell into the bay, where it sank

immediately. "Yes, that's true, she is, but she's not
an easy woman to get to know, Josh. She's very . . .
determined. She loves the piano, and since I don't, I
think she wrote me off a long time ago."

"But you're here helping her—"

"Which she expects and tolerates and detests, all at
the same time."

He smiled. "Your grandmother sounds like a tough
cookie."

"You could say that." I glanced at my watch and
took off Josh's jacket. "I've got to go."

He took the jacket. "So soon?"

I explained about the doctor's appointment, and was
secretly pleased he seemed genuinely disappointed I
was leaving.

"When will I see you again?" he asked.

I shrugged. "I don't know."

"I was thinking. I'm back and forth almost every
day, almost always around ten in the morning or one
in the afternoon. Maybe, if you have time, you could
meet me at the dock occasionally. I could call the house
and forewarn you—"

"If my grandmother answers the phone, don't tell
her who you are, okay? She would be terribly upset if
she thought I was conniving with the enemy behind
her back."

His eyebrows knitted together in the middle. "It's
that bad?"

"It's that bad."

"Okay, but if you get a message that your dry cleaning will be ready by such and such an hour, you'll know it's me."

I laughed. "Grandmother isn't senile," I said. "She's seen my wardrobe and knows perfectly well it's all wash and wear. Tell her you're an old friend."

"Instead of a new friend?" he asked with a terribly disarming smile.

"Right. I'd better go."

He nodded, and still we both stood there, the wind whipping our hair, the skiff bumping against the dock. I wasn't sure what either one of us was staring at, or how we'd gracefully stop staring; it was just that for a moment, the world narrowed down to his brown eyes and it was enough. Then he raised a hand and touched my cheek with his workingman's fingers. No touch had ever been as gentle.

"You'll hear from me," he said, and I nodded before turning around and walking quickly away.

Chapter Six

" "You're doing fine, Mrs. Brook-field, except your blood pressure is on the low side and you look a little pale to me. Are you resting and taking your medication?"

My grandmother said, "Of course I am."

"Hm—" Dr. Pullman said. "Well, it takes time. And you, young lady—are you making her take her naps, like I told you?"

Dr. Pullman didn't see the tight line my grandmother's lips formed or the irritated glance she threw in his direction. I meekly said, "Grandmother is a big girl, Doctor."

"Who needs to take care of herself," he said.

She looked at me, daring me to tell him about the

long piano lessons that had obliterated any chance for afternoon naps. I said, "I'm cooking very nutritious food."

He nodded thoughtfully. I glanced at Grandmother, and if I expected a grateful nod of her head, I was foolish. She expected me to support her, would have been shocked if I hadn't. For one thing, she didn't think I had the backbone to stand up to her. She didn't know I was fully aware that if we had ganged up on her to make her stop giving her lessons, she would have stewed and fought us to the point where she'd get even less rest than she was presently getting.

"Well, we'll see you again in a week, Mrs. Brookfield. Please, try to stay quiet. Use this summer to catch up on your reading. Let this pretty granddaughter of yours pamper you silly." He looked at me and wagged a finger. "Keep her quiet and rested; that's what older bones need, young lady."

Grandmother cast him a withering look as I helped her fit her loose-sleeved coat over the cast, then the arm into the sling. I think we both breathed a sigh of relief as we left the office.

"Did you hear that insipid music?" she demanded as I opened her door.

"I didn't notice," I said.

"*Beatles* tunes, watered down and commercialized till the life is wrung out of them! That man!"

I closed her door and walked around the big Pontiac.

It had leather upholstery, and had been sitting in the sun. As I opened the door and slid in behind the wheel, I took a deep breath and immediately thought of Josh.

We drove home in silence, stopping only once to pick up more food at the small neighborhood grocery Grandmother preferred. I let her choose what she wanted; her tastes ran toward seafood and pasta, paralleling my own. Eating seemed to be the one thing we had in common.

When the doorbell rang that night I almost leaped from the chair. Grandmother looked up from the book she was pretending to read while she dozed, and Caspar jumped down from the secretary where he'd been washing his snowy paws. Three days into the summer, and a ringing doorbell had become the big thrill of the evening.

"You get it," Grandmother ordered.

I put aside another one of her blouses and rose. The doorbell rang again. I couldn't believe my eyes when Gerald Holt faced me on the doorstep.

He put his fingers to his lips before I could call him by name. "Is she here?" he whispered.

I nodded, torn with indecision. No matter how much I liked Gerald Holt, my grandmother didn't. What right did I have to go behind her back to satisfy his wishes?

I opened my mouth, and he shook his head. "Just

let me come into the room," he begged, his voice very low. "Once she sees me—"

"Ellen?"

"Just a moment, Grandmother," I called over my shoulder. Then, turning back to Gerald, I said, "I'm sorry, but I can't—"

"Ellen?"

"Just a moment," I repeated. "Gerald, please. Trust me, this isn't the way. Give her a few days, a couple of weeks. You can't barge in—"

And then she was at my side, opening the door further, face-to-face with Gerald Holt.

"You!" she hissed.

"Mimi," he said softly. "Mimi, please, just let me talk to you—"

"I have nothing to say to you!" she snapped.

"But, Mimi, it's been fifty-five years—"

"I don't care if it's been one hundred and fifty-five years. Now, don't bother me again." She slammed the door with such force the windows rattled in their frames.

"Grandmother?"

She looked at me, her face flushed, her eyes blazing. And then I saw a tear roll down her wrinkled cheek. I reached out to comfort her, but she turned away from me and fled down the hall. Soon I heard another door slam. Caspar looked at me from underneath the sofa, his eyes round as saucers. I knew just how he felt.

And wasn't I doing a great job of keeping her rested and quiet?

I opened the door, hoping Gerald was still there so I could walk him down to the dock, hoping that at least he would allow me to help him, but he was gone and the sidewalk was empty.

The next day was as slow a day as I'd ever spent anywhere. In utter boredom, I mopped the clean kitchen floor and made an elaborate casserole for lunch, the aroma of which sent Caspar into feline ecstasy as he waited by the oven for my masterpiece to bake.

Rattling the timbers, so to say, was the sound of piano scales, repeated over and over again by a little blond girl named Kate or Karen who must have had three thumbs. The little girl was duly replaced by an older girl who at least could play, but, of course, Grandmother didn't think she was playing as well as she could have and pressured her incessantly to sit up straight, to not drag her fingers, to keep better time, to practice, practice, practice! My old insecurities sprang to life as I imagined what the poor kid was going through, and I tackled the messiest pans in the kitchen with a vengeance that resulted in some mighty clean copper bottoms.

The older girl finally left as the timer went off on the stove. "Lunch!" I yelled. If Grandmother could yell at me, I could yell at her.

She entered the kitchen, regal in purple, spine straight, head held high, the effect ruined only by the dark circles under her eyes that told the real story of the night she'd spent after Gerald's surprise visit.

I spooned scallops à la something onto our plates, putting a little aside in Caspar's bowl to cool. He howled in protest, but I took my cue from Grandmother and ignored him.

"I'm sorry about last night," I said as we began eating.

She looked at me. "Oh?"

"About Gerald Holt. I don't want you thinking I arranged that visit or had anything at all to do with it. I wouldn't go behind your back like that."

Grandmother looked as if she wanted to bolt again, but maybe one emotional outburst a week was her limit, and she'd already suffered two or three. She nodded stiffly. "Thank you, Ellen. I know my behavior must seem . . . strange to you, but it's simply the way it must be. I think Mr. Holt got the message last night. I don't think we'll have to concern ourselves with him again."

I wasn't so sure.

"This is very good, Ellen. Where did you learn to cook?"

An actual question? "Mom," I said.

This earned me a raised-eyebrow response. I knew Grandmother thought my mother was good for just about nothing, but had it really managed to escape her notice that my mother was a great cook?

"Her father was an accomplished chef," she said.

"Grandpa?"

She looked pained at my use of such a homey name for a man I'd never met, but for once she didn't put me in my place. "He was a very . . . capable man," she continued. "He could do anything better than anyone else."

Boy, they must have been a fun couple! I mused, thinking of my poor wispy mother, brought up in a house with two dynamos like that. No wonder she was content to flit from this to that. She'd probably never done anything good enough for either parent.

"Where are you going this afternoon?" Grandmother asked.

"Do you have lessons?"

"Five. All advanced."

I nodded, wishing I had the guts to try to make her slow down, knowing she wouldn't listen to me even if I did. Josh hadn't called, and I didn't want to wear out my welcome by calling him, so I really had nowhere to go. "For a walk," I said, knowing I couldn't stand to be in the house through five more lessons.

"That's too bad. One young man, Tyrone Rathers is his name, is quite good. If you stayed, you'd be treated to a nice rendition of Chaminade's 'Scarf

Dance.' She was a wonderful composer, don't you think?''

Leave it to Grandmother to try to have a musically literate conversation with her musically illiterate granddaughter. I said, ''Oh, yes. Yes, she was.''

''And Tyrone is such a wonderful young man. He's about your age, Ellen, an accountant with the state. Took up the piano a little late, but he's making splendid progress.''

''That's . . . good,'' I said.

''Perhaps you'll be home in time to join us for sherry or a cup of tea?''

''Maybe. Maybe I should set everything out before I leave in case I'm not.''

She nodded. ''I was in your room yesterday, looking for a certain music book, and I couldn't help but notice the picture on your nightstand, the one of the young man.''

''Danny Gorman,'' I said.

''Is he your boyfriend?''

Was my grandmother actually trying to set me up with a piano-playing accountant?

''Because if he's just a friend, as you young people say nowadays, I would like to introduce you to Tyrone. He's a sensible man from a good family. I don't know why some girl hasn't already snatched him up.''

As uncertain as I felt about Danny, I said boldly, ''Danny and I are engaged, Grandmother.'' That ought to put an end to any romantic thoughts she had of me sitting side by side on the piano bench with Tyrone Rathers.

She shook her head. "Engaged? Why didn't your mother tell me?"

"Because," I said, trying to think why, "because it all happened very suddenly, and Mom doesn't know yet. Let's just keep it to ourselves."

Grandmother rose. "What does an engagement really mean, Ellen? It's a promise, that's all, and a promise is only as good as the people who make it."

"Are you saying my word is no good?" I asked. Was the woman a mind reader? Did she somehow sense the ambivalence I felt about Danny?

"I'm not saying *your* word is no good, no. But take my advice, young lady. Until you see a gold band around your finger, don't take anything for granted."

"You're right, I suppose."

"Of course I'm right."

"I mean, Danny and I have been dating for a year or so. When I told him I was coming up here to help out, we sort of decided we'd probably get married this next winter. Or maybe in the spring."

"That's just what I mean."

"Yes, well, the whole thing is okay with me. I agree with Danny."

"Then you'd be willing to spend an evening with Tyrone?"

"No, that's not what I mean."

Grandmother thumped her fingers against the back of the chair. I was already regretting this spontaneous fictional engagement. "An engagement was a serious thing when I was a girl," she said, looking over my head. "One did not break an engagement easily."

"Well, I'm not exactly breaking an engagement, am I? You wanted to know if Danny and I were serious about each other, and the answer is yes." Boy, would Danny be shocked to hear me say all this; he and Susie were probably married by now.

Grandmother nodded. We were both saved any further discussion when the doorbell rang. As I left to admit the first victim of the afternoon, I saw Caspar jump onto the table and polish off Grandmother's lunch while she absently ran her hand along his spine. She didn't feed him *from* the table; she fed him *on* the table!

A klutzy rendition of Strauss's "On The Beautiful Danube" got me through the dishes and out the door in record time. It was chilly today, and I wrapped my sweater around me as I walked. Of course, I walked toward the bay, hoping I'd run into Gerald or Josh, hoping everything was okay.

Their dock was empty of boats, and if I squinted, I could make out three boats tied to the Oyster Island dock. What was unsettling was the way I wished I was over there with them. That island seemed more real than my grandmother's house; the men and the dog who lived there already seemed like old friends.

I was still a little shaken by the lunchtime conversation, regretting the lie I'd told to spare myself and Tyrone Rathers an uncomfortable evening. Now Grandmother thought I was engaged, and apparently this was a matter she had ambivalent feelings about. What would she think of me in a year or so when I was still unmarried? Well, what did I care?

But I did care, and that was unsettling too.

I stood around on the dock for a while till it got too cold, then I began walking around the old town, finally winding up in front of the same jewelry store—Nature's Gems—as a couple of days earlier. The window still had the HELP WANTED sign in it, but what caught my eye was a beautiful necklace of freshwater pearls. I went inside.

A woman sat behind the counter on a stool, eating a bagel, reading a magazine, something I had done myself on slow days back in my own shop, back in my real life.

She looked up and smiled. "May I help you?"

"Slow day," I said.

"You'd better believe it. But it's summer, and any moment, a whole car full of wonderful tourists might barge through that door and demand a hundred things."

We both laughed. "I was admiring the necklace in

the window," I told her. "The three strands of fresh-water pearls with the gold-tone beads."

"That's a beauty."

"How much do you want for it?"

"Sixty-nine dollars."

"Not a bad price." Trouble was, I could get it my-self, wholesale, for half of that. But were there any in the store, and if it had to be ordered, would Susie be willing to do it for me and then ship it up by late August when Grandmother celebrated her seventy-sixth birth-day?

"I like your shop," I said as I admired the glistening cases. The walls were covered with shelves, which were in turn covered with everything from books to huge chunks of sparkling amethysts, baskets of loose beads to racks of sterling-silver earrings. Several floor cases were arranged around the small room, giving the store a cluttered, but interesting, look.

She finished off her bagel and closed the magazine. "Thanks, but between you and me, I'm beginning to despise it. Harry quit last week, right at the beginning of summer, the louse, and now I can't even take a day off. No play, all work makes Bonnie a cranky girl."

Since Bonnie was about fifty, with gray curls and a lush figure appropriately decorated with numerous pieces of her own jewelry, I laughed again. "I know what you mean," I said.

"Do you have a store too?" she asked.

"Just about like this one, in Oakland. But I have two co-owners to share the load."

"And the profit."

"A trade-off."

"Yes."

I started to add something else, but just then the door opened, and three women came into the store. One asked Bonnie about the same necklace I'd inquired about, and the other two gravitated to one of the earring cases. Bonnie cast me an I-told-you-so look.

I occupied myself by admiring a case of museum replicas, especially the electroplated cartouche from Tutankhamen's tomb. I'd been a sucker for Egyptian jewelry since my mother took me to Seattle to see the touring exhibit of "King Tut" artifacts when I was a kid. I looked up as the bell on the door announced five more people. Bonnie was trying to answer three questions at once. She saw me looking and motioned for me to join her.

"Do you want the freshwater-pearl necklace?" she asked.

"Go ahead and sell it," I told her.

She nodded and began ringing up the necklace.

"How much are these earrings?" one of the original women asked.

Bonnie said, "Just a moment, okay? I'll be right there."

"Then would you help me find a man's onyx ring?" another woman said.

A man cleared his throat. "I believe I was here first. I need to find a crystal for my daughter's birthday. She says there's one that's supposed to transmit healing energies. Something like that."

"Clear crystal," I said. "They're in the case right over there."

"About these earrings?"

The jingle of the door announced more customers.

"Would you like some help?" I asked Bonnie, who was just handing the boxed necklace and the change to the first customer.

"Really? Would you, honey?"

"Sure."

"Great. Help the gentleman, okay? I'll get the earrings. Here's the key to the case."

She tossed me the key, and I went to help the man find the proper crystal for his daughter's birthday.

By the time the rush was over, I'd sold two crystals (upon hearing rose quartz is supposed to promote tranquility, the man had bought a second crystal for his wife, and I'd considered buying one for my grandmother), an amethyst ring, a blue-topaz necklace, and an abalone watch. Bonnie sat back on her stool and said, "I don't even know your name."

"Ellen Nickleson." I extended my hand. We shook and exchanged silly grins.

"Well, Ellen, thanks. You've got a job if you want it."

I sighed. "I couldn't."

"Oh, I know. You have a shop in Oakland. I just wish you lived here, that's all. You're great."

"Actually, I'm here for the summer," I told her. If I walked by the shop often, she was bound to notice me. "I'm taking care of my grandmother."

"Then, why not work here too?" she asked, suddenly sitting upright.

"Well. . . ."

"Not every day."

"But—"

"I'd pay you whatever you want."

I laughed. "Just until you find someone permanent?"

"Of course."

"Because I can't promise what hours I'll be able to put in, and there may be days when I can't come at all. I'll be horrible to schedule around. Are you sure you want me?"

She reached across the counter and grasped my hand. "Honey, am I ever! And, tell you what—I have another pearl necklace in the back, one with four strands instead of three. You can have it at cost."

"I guess I'm hired," I said.

"I guess you are," she agreed, beaming.

Chapter Seven

The days fell into a pattern. Mornings, I either worked at Nature's Gems, or did housework while some beginning piano student wreaked havoc on my sanity. Afternoons, I either worked at Nature's Gems or did housework while some advanced piano student drove me nuts with Beethoven, Mozart, or Rachmaninoff. I'd expected my grandmother to be a little put out that I'd accepted a job without consulting her, but she'd accepted the news with little noticeable reaction. Perhaps she was as glad to have me spend part of the day out of her house as I was to go.

I liked working at the store, but I felt stranded, as though my life were an island and I was on a boat sailing away from it. The high point of each day slowly evolved into getting postcards from my mother, each with some beautiful French landmark, each saying, "Wish you were here." *She* wished I was there?

I knew she felt guilty for flying off when her mother needed her, guilty for leaving me with three months' worth of a job she herself would have hated.

Besides, and this was hard to admit even to myself, I didn't know why Josh didn't call. I mean, he was certainly under no obligation, but I jumped every time the phone rang, returning to that nervous state I'd thought I'd left behind in high school when Todd Bellamy put off asking me to the junior prom until four nights before the big event. I wanted to see Josh. I wanted to ask if Gerald was okay after my grandmother slammed the door in his face, wanted to make sure. But just as much, I wanted to look at Josh, listen to him, see his boats, eat lunch on his picnic table, get to know his silly mutt. I wanted to go to a movie with him, drive into the country, walk on a beach. I didn't really know him yet, and more than anything else, I wanted to.

Only, I reminded myself five hundred times a day, I was supposed to want to do these things with Danny Gorman.

I returned from the store late one afternoon three weeks after coming to Eureka, over two weeks since last seeing Josh, to find Grandmother waiting for me in the kitchen. She'd been growing steadily stronger, though by this time of day she tended to look a little wilted, like a flower plucked from the vine and plopped in a crystal vase where its stem couldn't quite reach the water.

I started a pot of water for tea as soon as I took off my coat, and I made her sit down. "It's time to take a pill," I told her as I shook one into my palm.

"Yes, yes. Ellen, a young man called here."

"An old friend?" I asked hopefully, handing her the pill and a small glass of cranberry juice. I was thinking of Josh, of course.

"Your fiancé."

"Danny?"

"Yes, and he said he wants to meet me."

"Grandmother," I said, leaning toward her, "you didn't say anything about our . . . our engagement . . . did you?"

"I congratulated him, of course," she said, after she swallowed the pill.

I smiled weakly. "What did he say?"

"He said, 'Thank you. It's most stimulating.' He has a very nice voice, Ellen. Most trustworthy."

The tea kettle started whistling. As I poured hot water into two mugs I wondered what Danny must think. I'd have to call him.

"And I signed up a new student today," she continued.

"Grandmother," I admonished, setting the tea in front of her, "what am I going to do with you?"

She straightened her spine. "I beg your pardon?"

"Your schedule is already so full."

"He's a beginner."

"But that means the morning, and you already have more lessons than—"

"He's coming at night. Now, I won't talk about it, Ellen. My life is my life. You may cook and clean for me, but I won't tolerate your interfering with how I make a living. I will not be an idle widow living off Social Security, not yet, anyway."

"I don't want you to be idle—"

"Well, that's good, then, isn't it? What's for dinner?"

She could change directions so fast! "Leftovers," I said, suddenly tired. I could hardly wait to get dinner over and Grandmother settled so I could doze off in front of the fire that she insisted I build every night, no matter how unbearably hot the room became. I'd almost grown used to fanning myself as I read. What in the world would I be like in another two months?

"That's fine. My new student will be here promptly at seven o'clock."

"Tonight?"

"Of course. I think I'll go put a match to the fire

you set in the grate this morning, then prop my feet up while you make dinner. Will that make you happy?''

Only if you torch the piano while you're at it, I thought as I dutifully carried her tea into the drawing room.

I heard the doorbell ring right at seven. I let Grandmother answer it while I escaped to my bedroom with the phone. The thin walls didn't do much to cut out the racket the new student was making—he (I could hear a deep voice) was worse than any of the others—so I dialed Danny's number and stood in the closet where it was almost quiet enough to hear.

''Hello?''

For a second I couldn't think what to say, because I thought I had dialed the wrong number. ''Susie?''

''Yes, this is Susie. Is this Ellen?''

I laughed. ''Of course. I'm sorry, I was trying to dial Danny's number. My mind must have slipped into overdrive and I called you instead. Anyway, how are you? Wow, it's good to hear your voice.''

''Hm—'' she said. ''Actually, Ellen, you did dial Dan's number. I'm over here having dinner.''

''Oh, I see.''

There was an awkward silence. Then Susie said, ''Should I get him for you?''

''Please. But first, how's the shop?''

''Oh, it's great. Melissa's friend Lynn is in town,

and she's been helping out. She's really terrific. Don't worry about a thing—we hardly know you're gone. I'll get Dan. Hold on.''

''Sure—'' But she was gone and I could hear her calling Danny to the phone. He picked up an extension.

''Hello, Ellen. How are you?''

''I'm fine. Susie tells me you're cooking dinner for her.''

''Veal scallopini. Did your grandmother tell you I called?''

''Yes, and I want to say I'm sorry about the mix-up.''

There was a long pause. ''What mix-up?''

''You know, she told you congratulations?'' Was he going to make me say it? Was he going to make me admit I'd told my Grandmother we were engaged?

''I thought it was nice of her to congratulate me on getting the Halverson job. What are you talking about, Ellen?''

''Nothing,'' I said quickly. Of course he'd thought her congratulations referred to the Halverson job. I hadn't even remembered his promotion. Some girl-friend I was.

''I called because I wanted to know what you did with the tickets we bought in April, you know, the advance seats for the concert at the civic center.''

''The concert that's next week,'' I said. ''I forgot all about it.''

"That's what I thought. Well, since you're up there and the concert's down here, do you mind if Susie uses your ticket?"

"No."

"So, where are the tickets?" he asked again.

"They're in my desk drawer at work. Tell Susie to look in my daybook toward the back."

"Great. Well, hang in there, Ellen. Your grand-mother sounds like a real doll."

"A real doll," I repeated. "Danny, don't take this wrong, but aren't you and Susie spending a lot of time together?"

He laughed. "Now, I wouldn't expect that kind of thing out of a modern woman like you," he said.

"What kind of thing?"

"Jealousy! I'll talk to you later."

"Don't hang up, Danny. I'm not jealous."

"Of course you're not. Listen, Susie says the sauce is burning, I have to go."

"Then go," I said, and hung up the phone.

Truth of the matter was this: In the back of my mind, I'd intended to tell Danny we were through. It wasn't as though he hadn't been telling me the same thing in a roundabout way, but I have found in life that it is much easier to dump a man than be dumped! But now, hearing his voice, remembering the concert and the grand plans we'd made to dress up and do the town before and after, knowing he had replaced me within hours and with a woman who was my friend—well, all this hurt.

In the space of ten minutes, I'd discovered that the shop didn't miss me, and that my boyfriend was dating my coworker. And not only had he *not* begged me to find a way to come south for the concert, he hadn't even offered to reimburse me the twenty-five dollars I was out on the ticket! Then, to top it off, he said I was jealous!

Was I?

I marched out to the kitchen and thumped the phone down on the counter so hard it squeaked in protest. I paced up and down the linoleum as the new student banged on the ivories and Grandmother admonished, "Please, play softer. There is no need to attack the keys."

Sure there is! I thought. I finally went outside and sat on the back steps with Caspar. He seemed content to watch a steady stream of ants whose route bypassed the sidewalk, so I watched too. When that grew old, I went back inside and resumed pacing.

Then I heard his voice.

"I'm sorry, Mrs. Brookfield. It's been twenty-one years since my last lesson."

Josh!

"That's quite all right, Mr. Smith. Now, start again."

As he played, and I use the term loosely, I tiptoed

toward the music room and sneaked a peek around the corner. Both backs were to me. All I could see of the man at the keyboard was a dark head and a red flannel shirt. I ducked out of sight as Grandmother said, ''I think that's enough for tonight,'' her voice as tight as the piano wires.

''I'll get better,'' the man said. There was no doubt in my mind that it was Josh's voice I was listening to. What in the world was he doing here?

''I am sure you will. No, don't pay me yet. Let's have another lesson first, shall we?''

''Tomorrow night?'' he suggested, and I could imagine my grandmother wincing at the mere thought of enduring forty-five minutes of his playing two nights in a row. I almost felt sorry for her. Not only was he as bad as her worst student, he was twice as loud too!

''I am not sure what good two successive nights will serve,'' she said.

''How about that recital in August?'' he persisted. ''Come on now, Mrs. Brookfield. Over the phone, you dangled the recital like a carrot in front of my nose.''

I think my mouth fell open.

''Then you'd better come tomorrow night,'' Grandmother said with an audible sigh.

Their voices had been coming closer, so I retreated back to the kitchen and came forward as though just finishing the after-dinner chores.

''Ellen, this is my new student, Josh Smith.''

Josh held out his hand. I shook it without meeting his gaze, but before I'd lowered my eyes, I'd seen the way he'd parted his hair down the middle and perched a pair of wire-frame glasses on his nose. "Nice to meet you," I said.

"You too," he said. "Thanks, Mrs. Brookfield. I'll see you tomorrow night."

Grandmother opened the door, and Josh looked at me. I saw the twinkle in his eyes, but I managed to keep my own expression neutral. "He seems nice," I said as Grandmother closed the door.

She sighed deeply. "He's a nice boy, but absolutely dismal at the piano. His hands are awfully big, but his fingers are nimble, if a little callused. He's got good, strong forearms, but I think he may be tone-deaf. Well, he'll learn; they always do. Ellen, if you don't mind, I'm going to bed. No, you don't need to help me. I'm quite capable of managing things by myself."

"Okay. I'm going outside to . . . to find Caspar . . . and then I may take a walk. Are you sure you're okay for the evening?"

She waved her good arm. I slipped out the front door as she walked down the hall toward her bedroom.

Josh was waiting down the block, where he'd parked his truck, standing on the sidewalk, leaning back against the front fender, arms across his chest. It was still light outdoors, of course, so I saw him straighten

up and face me. He'd finger combed the part out of
his hair.

"It's good to see you," he said, taking my hand,
and I felt myself smile from the inside out. In the house,
I'd been irritated with him for breaching Grandmother's sanctuary. But out here, I couldn't help but feel
pleased to see him, the same way I might feel upon
meeting an old friend who'd been away, one I'd been
secretly afraid I might never see again.

"Mr. Smith, I presume? Where are the glasses?"

"In the truck. Listen, will you take a drive with me,
Ellen? I think we need to talk."

"I think you're right." I climbed into the truck,
taking care not to sit on "Mr. Smith's" glasses.

He drove across the bridge that connected Eureka
with the Samoa Peninsula. We didn't say much as he
drove. We traveled down the peninsula for a while,
then pulled over and parked next to the wide sand
dunes. "How about a walk?" he suggested.

"It's a little chilly," I noted. "I came without a
coat again. Not even a sweater this time."

He took a thick wool sweater out from behind the
seat. "How about this?"

"That will be fine." I pulled the fisherman's-knit
sweater over my head. It smelled like wood and cars,
not entirely unpleasant. We walked across the dunes
until we reached the beach. The sun was low to the
horizon, and for a second I was worried about how

we'd find our way back to the truck in the dark, but then I figured a man like Josh wouldn't get lost on a beach. He gestured south and we began walking, the cold breeze at our backs.

"What were you doing in my grandmother's house?" I asked.

"Taking a lesson, obviously."

"Under an assumed name and with a silly disguise that wouldn't fool a soul."

"I thought she might have seen me the night I came to the house with Granddad."

"She didn't."

He stopped walking, caught my arm, and turned me to face him. "You're angry," he said.

"Wouldn't you be? She's made her feelings about your grandfather crystal clear. What do you hope to accomplish by sneaking around on her blind side, buttering her up? Eventually, you're going to have to tell her who you really are, and then, Josh, she's going to hit the ceiling."

"Your grandmother struck me as a very civilized woman."

"You don't know her. What you got tonight was her teacher mode. Come up on her personal side, and I guarantee she'll hack you into little pieces."

He looked down at the sand. I resumed walking. The sun was making its nightly plunge into the ocean, painting the sky orangy pink and the high scattered clouds deep purple in the process. Such a gaudy show.

"Wait," Josh said as he caught up with me.

We walked awhile in silence as the ocean waves crashed off to our right, the foam hissing in the semi-dark.

"It wasn't my idea," he said at last.

"Let me guess—your grandfather again?"

"I'm afraid I let him talk me into this ruse as a sort of last-ditch effort. I had to do something. He sits around and stares at things or walks all over that island into the wee hours of the morning. It's as though he's obsessed. I refused this whole idea at first, but he threatened to go back to Ohio, so I finally gave up and called your grandmother. I couldn't tell her who I really was, of course."

"Would it really be so awful if Gerald did go back to Ohio?" I asked gently.

"There's no one left in Ohio. He had two sons, and they're both dead. I'm the only grandchild. He doesn't like my mother and she doesn't like him. All my grand-mother's family is dead or scattered. What's in Ohio for him? And who will watch out for him?"

"Does he need watching out for?"

"Two weeks ago I would have said no. Now? He doesn't sleep, he doesn't eat. Something is gnawing away inside him. Something is making him miserable, and every indication is that it's your grandmother. So I signed up for lessons.''

''I suppose he told you about coming to the house unannounced? I thought it was quite romantic, but Grandmother was absolutely livid.''

Josh shook his head. ''I was so mad at him when he told me what he'd done.''

''Why were you angry at him?'' I asked, struggling to see his face in the gathering dark. ''He didn't do anything wrong, not really. It was a little foolhardy, knowing my grandmother, but hardly criminal. He just wanted to see her.''

''I'm not very proud of this, Ellen. When he told me what he'd done, how he'd tried to get you to sneak him inside, and how your grandmother slammed the door in his face, all I could think of was that maybe you were mad too, maybe you wouldn't want to see me again. See any Holt man, for that matter. Can't say as I'd blame you.''

''So that's why you haven't called?'' He nodded, and I just laughed, mainly to myself. Here he'd been worrying about the same things I'd been worrying about, only backward or something. I touched his arm. ''Josh—''

''It's okay, Ellen. I don't know, maybe I let myself be talked into this piano-lesson thing so that I could see you. All I know for sure is that Granddad has been growing steadily more preoccupied. How about your grandmother? Is she unhappy too?''

I thought for a second. ''You know, I do believe she's actually been a little easier to get along with since that night. That doesn't make any sense.''

Suddenly, a wave sneaked up on us and broke close to where we were standing. I saw the flash of white foam too late, and the cold spray caught me as I dashed for higher sand. I heard Josh running behind me.

He laughed as we both stopped running. ''Are you soaked too?'' he asked.

''Yes, way past my knees. How about you?''

''I squish when I walk,'' he said. ''Come on.''

I trudged up the beach behind him, toward the dunes, stepping over dark shapes that looked like dead seals and birds from a distance, but always turned into driftwood, thank goodness.

It was almost dark. Josh said, ''Why don't you sit down for a moment?'' and I gratefully sank down beside a beached log. My sneakers were soaked, and my salty, cold, stiff, wet jeans clung to my legs.

Josh reappeared, his arms full of something. ''What are you doing?'' I asked as he dropped to his knees beside me.

''Building a fire.'' He opened his arms and the small pieces of driftwood clattered onto the sand.

''Just like that?''

''Well, it's dark, so it's hard to see how wet the

wood is, and I have only three matches and no paper, so I wouldn't exactly say, 'Just like that.'"

But in the end, it all happened as I imagine the Boy Scouts manual says it's supposed to. The little wood caught fire and ignited the big wood, and I got so close I could smell my jeans steaming.

"Wonderful," I said, holding my hands close to the flames. The wind seemed to shift every thirty seconds, so the only trick was staying out of the smoke.

"I should have talked to you first," Josh said, as he unlaced his sneakers. He propped them against a rock next to the fire and wiggled his toes in the sand.

"Talked to me about what?"

"About the plan to invade the Brookfield house, to get to know your grandmother. I've put you smackdab in the middle, and I'm sorry."

I sat down next to him. "It's okay."

He took my hand and studied my fingernails. "No, it's not. You told me weeks ago that you didn't want to sneak around behind her back, but that's exactly what's going to happen. By pretending to accept me as Josh Smith, you're in on it."

"It's okay," I repeated.

"So you're not mad?"

"No, I'm not mad. I'm confused and worried about where this is all going to end and how many people are going to wind up getting hurt, but I'm not mad. I can see where Gerald could wear a man's resistance down.''

He laughed softly, to himself. ''It seems as though I'm always doing the wrong thing and apologizing for it later.''

''You're just trying to help your grandfather,'' I said. He was rubbing my fingers with his thumb, and it was doing all sorts of funny things to my insides. Part of me said I should take my hand away. A bigger part told me to keep it right where it was.

''Are you still cold?'' he asked.

''Not too bad.''

''But you're shivering. You're trembling.''

I laughed softly, but when I looked at him, I saw him studying my face. His was half lit by the firelight, golden and mysterious, his eyes dark secrets. I felt his hand move up my arm, cup my chin, coax me closer till our lips touched and a thunderbolt passed between us.

We both drew away and looked at each other, and then we melted back together, and he was kissing me, and I was kissing him, and for a moment or two, the world existed only in that small flickering circle of light.

''Ellen,'' he whispered at last, running his fingers over my face, through my hair. ''Is there anyone else, Ellen?''

That called me back to reality! I caught his hand and

held it beneath his chin. "I don't think so," I whispered.

He drew away so he could see me. "What? What does that mean?"

"It means I've been going with Danny Gorman for about a year. I don't know where we stand right now, but I guess until I do, the right thing to do would be to stop kissing you."

"Under protest?" he asked as his lips brushed my neck.

"Under protest." I kissed his hand and said, "You might as well know the rest of it. My grandmother is under the impression Danny and I are engaged to be married."

"And how did she come to be under that impression?"

"I sort of told her. It's all very complicated."

Josh laughed dryly. "Great. It looks like winning your heart is going to be as tricky as everything else lately. Makes a fellow think he should stay on his island and be content just to build his little boats."

"Promise me you won't be a quitter," I said slowly as the wind changed direction and blew smoke into our faces.

"I promise," he said.

Chapter Eight

661 want something made out of peacock feathers," the man said. He was about fifty, with a shiny bald head and a round stomach that threatened to pop the buttons on his heavy cardigan. Eureka was having a typically foggy morning; I even had the heater turned on to keep the store warm.

"We don't have a lot," I warned him as I led him to the case in the corner. "We have wire earrings and a barrette. Oh, this headband is either pheasant or peacock. Yes, it's peacock."

He picked up the headband. "It's for my wife," he explained. "Her family had peacocks when she was growing up, and she's always wanted something made with their feathers. But she wouldn't like the idea that something was killed just to get feathers for her.''

''The birds weren't killed for their plumage,'' I assured him. He put the headband back and picked up one of the earrings, a softly fringed blue, green, and brown feather dangling from a French wire. ''Those are beautiful,'' I said.

''I like them. How much?''

''Ten dollars.''

He nodded. ''Okay. Wrap them up.''

I wrapped them up and sat down on the stool as he closed the door behind him. I was in a sour mood because a week of piano lessons had passed and I still didn't know what to do.

The thing was, Grandmother *liked* Josh. She really liked him. She tolerated the most awful chords from his clumsy fingers, and that alone, even without the fact that she never really yelled at him, was a dead giveaway about how she felt. It was going to break her heart when she found out who he was.

Unless . . . I thought, suddenly sitting upright.

A jingle on the door announced another customer. I tore myself from my private musing, resenting the fact that my plotting was being interrupted before it was complete, and looked up to find—

''Grandmother!''

''Ellen. So this is the little shop you work at.''

My surprise at seeing her in the shop was doubled

when she tugged on the arm of the red-haired man who accompanied her and said, ''Tyrone, this is my grand-daughter.''

He was about the same height as my grandmother, with a medium build similar to Danny's. He had wavy hair and lovely green eyes, and his hands were fine boned and sensitive looking. It was easy to imagine those hands darting about a keyboard, hitting the right notes, pleasing my grandmother.

''I've heard a lot about you,'' he said as we shook hands.

I nodded, darn near speechless. Grandmother looked at the two of us with manipulation in her eyes; I wondered if Danny had called again and spilled the beans, telling her we were no more engaged than we were flying to the moon.

''Tyrone needs a birthday gift for his dear sister, so I suggested he drive us down here. I know you can help him.'' She patted Tyrone's arm and added, ''Ellen is very clever that way.''

''I'll . . . I'll be glad to help,'' I stammered. My grandmother was actually being coy!

''She likes bright things,'' Tyrone said, smiling shyly. I had the impression he was aware of what Grandmother was doing, but whether he was in cahoots with her or was simply another helpless victim was anyone's guess.

I decided to be businesslike. ''As in gemstones?''

"Not that expensive," he said. Grandmother frowned at him, and I secretly smiled.

"I have a red-jasper pendant back here. It looks kind of like a doughnut suspended on a black cord. Very modern. I think it costs about thirty dollars."

Tyrone glanced nervously at my grandmother, then at me. I said, "Wait, even better! How about these cute little handcrafted clay earrings? Or this, my favorite." I held aloft a pin, the size of a doughnut hole, composed of one red strawberry, green leaves, and three white flowers. The price tag—$7.50—dangled where Tyrone could see it.

"That's cute," he said. He patted his pocket and added, "I left my checkbook in the car. Will you hold it for a few minutes while I run and get it?"

"Of course." I took it back to the counter. Grandmother was perched on the stool, clutching the counter with one hand to balance the cast on the other. As usual, she looked stunning, this time in a deep-red sweater with very full sleeves, her sling fashioned from a jazzy flowered scarf I'd spent half an hour that morning folding and pinning.

"I didn't know he was so cheap," she said as Tyrone closed the door behind him.

"Grandmother!"

"He didn't have enough in his wallet for that little trinket? How much is it, anyway?" She grabbed for the strawberry, but I snatched it away.

"None of your business. Why did you really bring him down here?"

She looked over her shoulder, saw the coast was clear, and said, "It occurred to me that your fiancé hasn't been to visit you once in the five weeks you've been here. You've got all your eggs in one basket, Ellen. Not a good idea."

This from the same woman who had told me how sacred an engagement was!

"I am not interested in Tyrone," I said firmly.

"Of course not. The boy might play the piano well, but I've just discovered that away from the keyboard, he's a twit."

"That's not it, Grandmother—"

"Then you're so in love with that Danny of yours that you can't see straight." I was surprised at the tender tone of her voice. Surprised? I was shocked. "It's not good to be that much in love, Ellen, trust me. Until he slips that ring on your finger, keep your eyes open."

"Grandmother—"

"Trust me on this," she said softly as the door opened and Tyrone strode across the shop, checkbook in hand. I thought I heard her add, "I know what I'm talking about," but she suddenly became quite interested in a case of silver bracelets, and I wasn't sure.

* * *

I walked home that afternoon, my mind a whirlwind. If my main concern was making sure Grandmother didn't kill Josh when she learned who he was, or more important, who he was related to, then I had to solve the Gerald/Naomi—or, rather, Gerry/Mimi—problem myself. Soon too, before he confessed, before she found out some other way, before it all came unglued. I had to find out what broke them apart, and then figure out how to get it all back together.

My motives were threefold and not entirely unselfish. I was growing fond of my grandmother, a fact that was a huge shock. I was worried about Gerald—if he was half as bad off as Josh said he was, then something had to be done right away. And third, I couldn't forget the memory of Josh's lips, or the feel of his arms, the way the firelight danced across the angles and planes of his face, or the way he'd said he wished we'd met a different way.

But how to go about it?

"One-two, one-two," Grandmother said sternly. I was sitting in the drawing room, waiting for Josh's lesson to conclude. Caspar was on my lap, kneading his claws into my leg, his eyes closed, his face turned to the fire, soaking up warmth. I was beginning to believe Grandmother: This cat was remarkably dull.

I was finally getting used to the noise of inexperienced fingers pounding on the wrong keys, and sometimes I could actually filter it out.

"That's enough, Mr. Smith," Grandmother said. "Let's try page forty-two in our John W. Schaum piano course."

A rustle of pages, then Josh saying, " *'Monkey Business'*?"

"That's correct. Now remember, one-two-three-four, one-two-three-four."

I winced as Josh banged out the notes, more or less, of a song I'd learned from the same book, as had my mother before me. Grandmother didn't seem to believe in updating her course books; in fact, when they went out of print, she photocopied copies for her students!

Bored, I picked up my mother's latest postcard, this one decorated with a picture of a cathedral at Chartres. *Wish you could have been here with us,* she wrote on the flip side. *Ellie, will you run over to the house and check on the Lamoreauxs? Make sure they're feeding Goofy. Thanks, honey. And, Mother, I hope you're feeling better. See you both in six weeks.*

I looked up when I realized it was silent. I stuck the postcard in my pocket and went into the music room to investigate.

"That's it, right there," Josh was saying. The room was dim, lit only by the drawing-room light that spilled across the threshold into the music room. Josh and Grandmother were standing at the tall window, he on her left side, away from her cast. Their heads were twisted sideways, their necks craned as they looked through the window.

"The little one?" she asked.

"That's right. The one right above the middle star in the handle of the Big Dipper. That's Alcor."

"And the Arabs used to test their eyesight by trying to find that star?"

"That's what my gr—that's what I've heard."

"But it's easy to pick out! And out on the desert, with no lights to fade the sky—why, that's too easy!"

He laughed. "Maybe it wasn't a contest, Mrs. Brookfield."

"My dear young man, everything is a contest."

"Even love?" he asked her softly.

"Especially love," she answered swiftly.

He laughed again. "Well, I still like Alcor. In fact, I think if I ever have a baby girl, I'll name her that. What do you think?"

"Alcor Smith," she said. "There wouldn't be two in a classroom. Let's just hope your future wife has some common sense and insists upon a pretty name like Amy or Linda."

Josh turned away then and saw me.

"I didn't mean to eavesdrop," I apologized.

Grandmother twirled around. "Nonsense, you're not eavesdropping. Mr. Smith was showing me a star." She switched on the lamp.

"I heard. Is your lesson over?"

Grandmother nodded. "Yes, I believe it is."

"I just wanted to tell you that I have to run over to Mom and Dad's house to check on Goofy. I'll be back in a little while."

"May I give you a lift?" Josh asked as he picked up the piano book and a few loose papers.

"That would be nice," I said.

Grandmother nodded. "Mr. Smith, now you practice! I really don't believe you're practicing a bit. An hour every day."

"I'll try," Josh promised.

"Fine. I'm going to read for a while, Ellen. Don't hurry back, I'm fine." She looked at Josh and added, "Ellen is a wonderful cook. I bet I've put on five pounds since she got here."

Josh gave her a once-over. "Looks good to me," he teased, and my grandmother—the woman who would barely speak a few weeks before; the woman with absolutely no sense of humor; the woman who fed the cat off the table, then belittled me for handing him a scrap—that very same woman almost giggled!

"Let's go," I said.

Josh was very quiet as we drove. I told him this after I directed him down a twisty side street that led to my parents' house.

"I've been thinking. I like your grandmother," he said.

"Of course you do. She wants you to like her, so she's charming."

"Yeah, well, she's going to hate me in a couple of weeks when Granddad shows up for a lesson with me. That's his newest plan."

"She'll throw a fit. I don't suggest surprise."

He turned off the engine. "What do you suggest?"

"I'm going to find out what went wrong between them so long ago and see if I can't fix it," I announced. "Now tell me everything your grandfather has told you."

He sighed deeply and hooked his arms over the steering wheel. I tried to ignore him, tried to pretend he was just a body sitting there and that the sight of him frowning to himself, the sight of his arms flexing, the way he smelled, and the little knot of tension in his jaw meant nothing to me.

"He hasn't said much. He calls her Mimi, which implies a certain . . . relationship, a certain familiarity. He obviously cared—cares—for her. The way he told us he felt when he first saw her also implies a romantic link. Let's see. He's said things like, 'Why, why, how could it have happened?' Stuff like that, stuff that doesn't pin anything down."

I shook my head. "She hasn't said another word about him, though as I told you that night on the beach, she seemed to feel better after slamming the door in his face. She wouldn't talk about the little piano tied to the burgundy ribbon. I just don't have a clue. But you know what? There's a very old box of photos in my mother's bedroom. Maybe the Lamoreauxs wouldn't mind if I went inside the house and took a look.''

''Let's at least try,'' Josh said, but he hesitated. At last he added, ''I was just thinking about that night on the beach. About the kiss, I mean. I didn't know about Danny. I wouldn't have—''

I touched his arm. ''I believe I was there too. I believe I was part of the kissing, and that if anyone should feel bad, it should be me.''

He looked at me, his eyes suddenly hard. ''And do you feel bad, Ellen?''

''No,'' I admitted, deciding on the spot not to mention the fact that I'd been trying to call Danny all week to let him know that as far as I was concerned, he was free to ride into the sunset with Susie. Josh had enough on his mind; besides, Danny was never home.

''Let's go see how they're treating Goofy,'' I said.

The Lamoreauxs turned out to be an attractive French couple in their mid-thirties—she with expertly dyed blond hair, he with a dazzling, warm smile, both of them with charming accents and a fairly good command of English. They recognized me at once, thanks to the shrine consisting of about three hundred pictures of Karen and me that my mother had constructed in the living room. The Lamoreauxs insisted we come in and check on Goofy for ourselves.

"Goofs!" I said as Mom's overweight dachshund waddled and panted his way toward me, his tail wagging furiously. I bent down and gathered the little hot-dog shape into my arms and tolerated a complete wash from the pink tongue.

"I couldn't imagine what a 'Goofy' was," Josh said as he patted the sleek brown head. "He's a cute little dog. Where did he get his name?"

"I'm afraid I named him," I admitted.

Madame Lamoreaux laughed. "He is a little go-getter, that one is." She was obviously delighted with Goofy. The dog wiggled his way out of my arms and into hers.

"Would you mind if I looked for something in my parents' room?" I asked.

"Oh, my dear, please, please, you must feel most welcome. This is your parents' home, is it not, and therefore, yours as well?"

I left the dog with her as I went into Mom and Dad's bedroom and crossed to the tall bureau.

It took me half an hour, and I had to dig through three shoe boxes of loose old photographs. Josh got bored halfway through and was now stretched out on the bed, staring at the ceiling.

"Josh?"

He sat up immediately. "Did you find something?"

"I think so. Go over to Dad's desk in the corner and see if he left his lighted magnifying glass. It should be right by the pencil sharpener."

"Here it is," he said, crossing the room, then dropping down onto the floor next to me. He looked at the five-by-seven black-and-white photo I held in my hand. "Is that it?" he asked.

"Look through the magnifying glass at her corsage."

He peered through the tiny lens, then wordlessly handed it to me. I did the same.

"Granddad's little piano is in the middle of the flowers," Josh said.

"But is this your grandfather?"

We both studied the tall young man standing next to Grandmother. He was handsome enough and his hair was thick enough, but over fifty years had passed. I wasn't sure I would have even recognized my grandmother if the picture hadn't been in my mother's collection.

"She looks a lot like you," Josh said.

"Grandmother? You're kidding! She's only about nineteen years old in this picture."

"Even so, she looks like you. I bet that someday when you're old you'll look the way she does now. But I don't think you'll have the frown lines she's got."

"What about the guy in the picture? Is it Gerald?"

"I think so. Is there anything written on the back?"

"Just a date: November twenty-ninth, 1934."

"A month to the day before Granddad married my grandmother."

"Six weeks before my grandmother married my grandfather."

Josh peered through the magnifying glass again, this time at the man's face. The two people in the photo were dressed formally, she in a beautiful lace dress, he in a dark suit. His arm was around her shoulders, and she leaned against him, smiling up into his face.

"It's him," Josh said. "I'm sure of it. See that little scar on his right temple? He got that when he was on the receiving end of a kick by an irate cow. He still has the scar."

"Well," I said, "at least our suspicions are confirmed."

"What do you mean?"

"Look at the way she's looking at him. They were in love, Josh."

"Yes," he said softly, looking at me now.

Then I looked back at the picture, and a creepy feeling sneaked up my spine. The feeling turned into a suspicion. "Is your grandfather out at the island? Would he still be awake?"

"I don't think he ever sleeps. Yes, I believe he's there."

"Can you take me to him? Right now?"

"Sure. What's wrong?"

"I have a feeling," I said as I looked at the picture. "I think I've had things turned around. Come on, let's go."

Chapter Nine

The bay was rough and the tide was going out, making the trip across to Oyster Island an adventure. The little motor sputtered and spat, but it pushed the boat forward across the chop. We passed all the boats in the marina, then had to skirt the edge of Woodley Island all the way down to the buoy, because Josh was concerned about the tide and the shallow water close to Woodley Island.

"All the lights are on at the house," Josh said. "Granddad should be there."

"Are the other boats at the dock? I can't tell."

"It would help if we had a full moon, but I think I see the tall shape of a mast and the bulk of the bigger motorboat."

He took the skiff north of his dock, cut the engine, and let the tide push him back into the float. I'd forgotten about Quincy, and almost jumped overboard when a silent black shape detached itself from the float and jumped into the boat, landing almost on my lap.

"Quincy!" Josh yelled.

The dog barked in my ear, then leaped out of the dinghy.

"Are you okay?" Josh asked. "I've got to break him of that habit."

"I'm fine." Now that the shock had worn off, I found myself laughing.

We tied up the skiff and Josh climbed out. He produced a flashlight from his pocket, and shined it on the float while he gave me a hand. I was pleased when he kept his hand firmly wrapped around mine as we walked up the ramp and down the dock.

"Low tide," he said.

"Is that why it stinks?"

"Stinks? I'll have you know what you smell is Humboldt Bay's finest marine mud, Miss Dry Land."

"It stinks to high heaven."

"Yeah, it does."

The yard light was on, illuminating the small yard in which five or six blades of grass attempted to hold at bay twenty acres of indigenous weeds. Off to the side, I could see the boat from the shed, outside now, a tall stick rising from its foredeck toward the stars overhead.

"Is the boat done?" I asked.

"Almost. Still a little interior work to be done and some of the rigging." He opened his front door and waited for me to enter.

The cabin was lit with kerosene lamps, which made the light more yellow than white. A small fire crackled in the fireplace. What we were in was a small living room cluttered with comfortable old furniture and worn rugs. Quincy darted through the open door and immediately went to a separate rug in front of the fireplace, where he promptly lay down, his gaze never straying far from Josh. There was no piano in sight; no wonder he never got any better.

"I like it," I said.

"Really?" Josh asked, and his question seemed sincere, as though my answer really mattered to him.

"I really do. It's warm and homey. That's a great print of an old clipper ship over the fireplace."

"It's not a print. Uncle Wes was a painter as well as a builder," he said as he threw another log on the fire and stabbed at it with the poker.

"Did he teach you about building boats?" I asked.

Josh leaned back against the mantel. "My dad died when I was a kid. I wasn't particularly good in school, and my mother couldn't seem to control me, so she shipped me out here to live with Uncle Wes. When I saw where he lived, I thought I'd died and been sent straight downstairs, you know what I mean? I was fifteen, still angry about losing my father, rebellious, scared, and I knew absolutely everything. No one could tell me anything. But Uncle Wes didn't try. He said something like, 'Well, let's make the best of this. Here's a list of your chores, there's a boat out front to get yourself to town every day to go to school, and if you need something, ask.'"

"And you liked it?"

"Not at first. At first I skipped school more days than I attended. Uncle Wes started taking me back and forth to Eureka, driving me to the school door, telling me frankly that I wouldn't have use of the skiff again until I straightened up, which I did right away because that boat was the only way for me to escape this island. And eventually, over the course of a few years, I found I didn't want to escape."

"You were content."

"Yep. I began reading up on boats and hanging around watching Uncle Wes fix old ones and build new ones. He started paying me to help him, so I read up some more, and pretty soon I was handling most of the work in the boat yard while he designed and built everything from sailboats to fishing boats. He built quite a name for himself in the process, as a man who could make a good, functional, and yet pretty boat. I still build his designs. I have his skills, but not his vision.''

Josh turned and looked into the flames. I could only imagine the grief he felt at losing a father twice, for that's really what had happened to him. I thought of my own father and the two or three times a year I saw him, and vowed to make it more often.

The fire popped embers onto the rug, and Josh stamped them out with the toe of his boot. He looked up at me and smiled, effectively melting my heart.

''You know, in Oakland, you'd die of heat prostration with a fire in the house in the middle of July,'' I said.

''I bet. Not here, though. We keep one burning all year long.''

''So does my grandmother. I bet that drawing room gets over a hundred degrees at times, but she refuses to go through an evening without a fire.''

Josh moved away from the fireplace and added, ''The island is the last place the fog burns off of in the morning, and the first place it returns to at night. I don't know if it's the proximity of the water or what, but it's always cool over here unless the sun is shining directly down and you happen to find a place out of the wind.''

While he spoke, he ducked his head into the other rooms, looking, no doubt, for Gerald, whom he seemed unable to find. ''Would you like a warm drink, or a cold one? I was thinking of brewing a pot of coffee.''

''Sounds good.''

He went off toward the kitchen, and I sat down near the blaze, Quincy by my feet. I felt totally at home, and I'm afraid my only thought of Danny was that I needed to get in touch with him and explain how I felt. That would give him the license to explain how he felt, and we could call it quits, nice and easy, no one hurt.

Unless I was reading more into this Susie thing than was really there. Unless his brisk manner was the same as his brisk manner always was. Danny had never been given to emoting much. He was of the stiff-upper-lip, squared-shoulders, emotions-contained school of thought. But I'd been telling myself for a year that that didn't mean he was devoid of emotions, just that he chose when and if to show them.

In all fairness, I reminded myself, we'd had our share of tender moments. Like the time he'd carried me across the street because I was wearing sandals and someone had broken a bottle on the pavement. Danny hadn't wanted me to cut my foot. Or the time he'd brought me a huge box of chocolates with a little note saying, *Sweets for the sweet*. Not terribly original, but nice. And I'd liked snuggling up to him, liked kissing him, liked making him smile.

Josh came back into the living room carrying two

steaming mugs, and it was suddenly as clear as a new day. I'd liked lots of things about Danny, but I hadn't ever loved him. And as Josh's hand touched mine, I realized there was a big difference between liking and loving.

We were on our second cup of coffee and I was thinking that brewing good coffee was not one of Josh's strong suits, when the door suddenly opened and Gerald came into the house.

He hung his jacket on a hook, then looked over toward the fire. He saw Josh first and tried to smile; then out of the corner of his eye, he saw me, and the smile, half formed, froze on his lips.

By now, I understood that time was flip-flopping on him again, and that the sadness in his eyes was not really meant for me. I stood and said, as un-Naomi-like as possible, ''Hi, Gerald. Have a nice walk?''

He cleared his throat. I was shocked at how he looked, as handsome as ever, but almost seedy: thinner, older, dark circles beneath eyes that were too intense. ''Ellen?'' he asked.

''Yes.''

He smiled ruefully, as though the joke was on him even though he couldn't possibly have read anything but acceptance and concern in Josh's or my eyes.

''A nice walk,'' he said.

''Where did you go, Granddad?'' Josh asked.

Gerald shrugged. "Out into the shrub, across the island. I was looking at the stars, just thinking."

I looked at his shoes and saw the soles were caked with mud. Gerald's gaze followed mine, and he kicked the shoes off by the door and crossed to the fire in his socks. He sat in a rocking chair, his gaze glued to me. It was a little unnerving.

"Ellen wanted to see you," Josh said.

Gerald looked at me as though remembering anew that I was Ellen, not "Mimi."

I said, "Yes, I did." I produced the picture of him and Grandmother, and set it on the table between us.

Gerald stared at the photo but said nothing.

"Granddad," Josh coaxed, "it's time you told us what's wrong. It's time we tried to help you fix it."

"There is no fixing it," Gerald murmured. "No, no fixing it at all."

"Maybe not," I agreed. "But something occurred to me tonight when I saw this picture. All along, I'd assumed Grandmother jilted you. How could I not? The woman has an iron will and, I thought, a heart of stone. But tonight, when I saw this picture, I noticed that she's gazing lovingly at you, but you're looking off to the side. Are you looking at someone else, Gerald?"

His gaze turned to me. I'd about given up hope that he would answer when he said, "Loretta. Loretta Pike."

"Grandma?" Josh said.

Gerald looked at his grandson. "Yes, your grandmother. I'd known her since she was a kid, a knock-kneed, freckle-faced kid. And then she came to the Grange Hall dance, the dance I'd brought my fiancée, Mimi, to, and I looked at Loretta and I realized she was all grown-up. I couldn't take my eyes off her."

Josh shook his head. "I don't understand."

Gerald shrugged. "The next day, Loretta's family moved in with my family. Their house had burned down, and they'd been staying in a hotel while it was being rebuilt, but when Dad found out, he insisted they stay with us. We had plenty of room, he said. But living like that with Loretta meant I got to know her. She was sweet and funny, and she made me feel wonderful. I fell in love with her, you see."

"But what about Naomi?" I asked.

He sighed so deeply I felt his distress in my own heart. "I guess I realized that I didn't love her the same way. I thought she was fascinating and beautiful, but she didn't seem to *need me,* if you know what I mean. . . ." His voice trailed off.

"So you broke up with my grandmother," I filled in for him.

He shook his head. "I didn't have the guts," he said bitterly. "We were engaged."

"But you didn't marry her," Josh pointed out.

Gerald sighed deeply. "No, I didn't marry her."

I looked at Josh, he looked at me, we both looked at Gerald, but he was slow to continue. At last he pointed at the photograph, at the corsage, and said, "I gave Mimi those flowers that night. Blue violets to match her eyes. I pinned the little piano onto it too, because she could play so beautifully. Have you ever noticed her hands?"

"Yes," I said softly.

"Beautiful hands," Gerald continued. "She loved the little piano, said she was going to keep it forever." He looked up at me. "But in the end, she returned it to me, and I couldn't blame her. I did love her, Ellen. Very, very much."

"When did you tell her about Loretta?" I asked.

"I didn't." He wiped tears from his eyes with trembling fingers. "I just didn't show up."

"You left her standing at the altar?" Josh asked, his voice as shocked as I felt.

Several seconds passed during which the hissing of the fire was the only sound in the room. Then Gerald nodded.

Poor Grandmother. Oh, the humiliation she must have endured!

Josh was out of his chair. He paced to the front door, then back again, his mouth a thinner line with each step he took.

"Loretta and I eloped," Gerald said woodenly. "She had family back in Ohio, so we went to live there. We got married, and a few years later, when war broke out, I enlisted in the Army and was shipped off to Europe.''

"How could you have done that to Mrs. Brookfield?" Josh exploded. "And Grandma! She knew all about it?"

Gerald nodded stiffly. I felt like curling into a little ball and hiding.

"I've never done anything I regretted more," Gerald said.

Josh stared at his grandfather, then shook his head. "No wonder the woman won't talk to you! And here I've been lying to her, taking those lessons, trying to find a way to insert your name, to get her to see you. . . ." He slapped his leg with his palm. "We've even involved her granddaughter in this charade, Granddad."

"I know, I know—"

"Ellen, I'm so sorry. I had no idea—" Josh began.

"Wait a second," I interrupted, realizing it was going to be up to me to mend things, or at least to try.

Josh stopped pacing and glared at his grandfather, who stared into the fire. Only Quincy looked content, his black fur glistening in the firelight, his ears cocked as he watched Josh.

"It was a terrible thing to do," I said slowly. "Obviously, it really hurt Grandmother, but it hurt you too, Gerald."

"I deserved every—"

"Just a minute," I broke in. "Let me finish. It hurt you too, but it was over fifty-five years ago, and you didn't exactly blight her life. She married my grandfather soon after you left, Gerald, and she had a daughter." I stopped talking because I wondered if what I was saying was really the truth. Had she married my grandfather on the rebound and suffered a loveless marriage? Maybe it didn't matter anymore, maybe that was the past and the future was what counted now. "You both led happy lives with other people," I continued. "You both had children. Sure, there was betrayal and pain, Gerald, but it's old betrayal and old pain."

"No, not old pain," Gerald said, his gaze still directed toward the fire. "I've regretted hurting her the way I did every day of my adult life. I was a coward with her, and no matter how many medals I went on to earn on the beaches of Normandy, I always knew it." He reached into his pocket and took out a familiar miniature piano trailing a scrap of faded ribbon. "I never saw Mimi again, not until the other night, that is. The only time I ever heard from her was when she sent this to my parents and they forwarded it to me in Ohio, and even then, there was no note, just the piano and the ribbon and an unspoken accusation."

Josh sat down opposite Gerald, resting his forearms on his legs and leaning forward. "What do you want of this woman, Granddad? Why can't you just leave her alone?''

Gerald looked up. ''Because I loved her, because I'm ashamed and guilty. Because I want her to forgive me.''

I sat back in my chair. Oh, dear. He wanted forgiveness, the one thing I had a feeling he would never get.

Gerald shook his head sadly. ''I'm thinking of myself again, aren't I? I've got you two kids lying to Mimi, I've got her remembering a painful past, all so I can ease my conscience.''

I didn't feel this was the right time to point out that, quite the contrary, Grandmother seemed to be enjoying whatever palpitations she was causing Gerald Holt's heart.

Josh said, ''Well, it's a mess, that's for sure, and I guess the one thing we can do to clean it up is to get out of this woman's life.'' I think he heard his own words, because suddenly he looked up at me, and I believe the same thought raced across his mind as raced across mine: Where did that leave *us?*

Chapter Ten

"I'll take you back to Eureka," Josh said.

"Do you think it's okay to leave Gerald alone?"

"I don't know."

We were standing outside on the dock. The sky overhead was cluttered with bright stars, and across the bay, the small city of Eureka looked like a colorful, twinkling metropolis. Josh and I stood close without touching.

"Don't be too angry at him," I said. "He was so young, and the voluptuous Loretta was right there under his nose—"

"Wait a second—that's Grandma you're calling voluptuous!" He shook his head. "You didn't know

Grandma, of course, but it's quite a stretch for me to think of her as the 'other woman.' '' He sighed, then he took my hand and raised it to his lips.

We walked down the dock carefully, because Josh had left the flashlight inside the house in the pocket of his coat. I thought it was probably near midnight by now, and the evening was strangely warm and soft.

''I should go back and get the flashlight,'' he said as I climbed down into the skiff.

''Do you want me to get it?'' I suspected the reason he didn't have his coat was that he'd left it hanging on the hook by the door, and now he was reluctant to go back inside and get it. It would probably do both him and Gerald some good to spend a little time apart right now.

''No, I don't need it to run you home and back.''

He climbed into the boat, and I guess instinct directed his hands, because a second later, the engine roared to life. We cast off the lines and started back across the bay.

We'd just made it to the buoy and were about to turn the boat and head north when the engine began sputtering, choking, finally coughing itself to death. Josh swore under his breath. The skiff immediately began heading south with the current.

''Grab the oars,'' he said as we both scrambled to find them. I felt one long shape and lifted it, turned it horizontal to the skiff (banging Josh on the head in the process) and tried to find the oarlock while Josh did the same with the other oar on the other side of the boat. I heard the clink of the metal probe as it hit the lock, and I thought I had the oar secured. I let go of it for just a second, and the next thing I knew, it had disappeared over the side.

''Change places with me and I'll row,'' Josh said. We were still heading south.

''I lost the oar,'' I confessed.

In retrospect, it was probably just as well that I couldn't see Josh's face. ''Change places anyway,'' he said after a moment. ''I'll have to paddle.''

So we gingerly changed places. We were almost opposite the long fish-buying docks now, and their lights spilled over onto the water a bit. The sight of Josh on his knees in the bow, paddling the skiff as though it were a canoe and he were some Alaskan guide investigating the wilderness, brought a smile to my lips that quickly turned into a giggle.

''What are you laughing at?'' he asked, peering at me over his shoulder.

I put my hand over my mouth. ''Nothing.''

To make a long story short, we ended up at the old boat harbor, the one used mainly by the fishing fleet. Josh had me hang on to a creosoted piling while he secured the skiff. I smelled like petroleum and dead fish by the time we climbed out of the skiff and began the long walk to my grandmother's house along fairly well-lit streets.

"I'm sorry about the oar." My apology was slightly weakened by the grin I couldn't seem to control. It was plastered to my face, and no matter how serious I tried to be, it kept playing around my lips.

Josh took my hand in his and smiled down at me. "Don't worry about it."

"I almost wish I could have seen your face when I told you I lost it. Your voice sounded really peeved. I mean, I don't really blame you, though you realize, of course, that it was purely accidental, but—"

"Ellen, what are we going to do about your grandmother?"

"We could tie her up and play elevator music until she agrees to talk to your grandfather."

"I have no idea what you're talking about. Will you please be serious?"

I giggled. "Listen, Josh, it's the middle of the night. I'm cold and tired and I smell funny, which tends to make me a little silly, and if you don't like it—"

He interrupted this speech with a prolonged kiss. "I like everything about you," he said. "Now, Ellen, what are we going to do? Should I stop taking piano lessons?"

"I don't know. Do you want to?"

"No, but I don't know why. I don't have a piano,

so I have nowhere to practice. I just like the nightly lesson. I like your grandmother. I like seeing you.''

''I like that too,'' I said. ''Can we talk about this tomorrow?''

''I even like the piano,'' he continued, ''and I do believe I'm getting better at it.''

Even tonight, even in the silly mood I was in, I knew not to touch that one.

''Will your grandmother accept me as Josh Holt? Should I simply confess and apologize? You know how good I am at apologizing.''

''She'll kill you and then she'll kill me. We'll have to be content to be disowned, disinherited, disliked.''

''Ellen, will you be serious?''

I stopped walking. ''No. I'm tired of being serious. I'll be serious tomorrow, but tonight I'm just going to be silly.''

''Then we'd better hold this conversation tomorrow.''

''What a good idea. Why didn't I think of that?''

He put his arms out as though to enfold me in a tender embrace—an idea that appealed to me—but when I moved closer, he hefted me up and threw me over his shoulder like an ungainly sack of potatoes.

After I stopped laughing, I rather enjoyed the ride.

''Ellen?''

''What?'' I mumbled.

"Ellen, wake up. It's me. Why is Mr. Smith asleep on the drawing-room sofa?"

I sat up. "Mr. Smith? Oh, that's right. Well. . . ." Here I stumbled. If I told her about the boat, she might put two and two together. Surely she knew Gerald's son had owned the boat yard on Oyster Island; she was probably aware that his grandson owned it now.

"Ellen?"

"His car broke down," I blurted out.

"Couldn't he just take a cab home? Is he as cheap as Tyrone?"

"I don't know," I said, actually ready to laugh. Grandmother had some strange conceptions. "I don't think so. I just offered him your sofa until morning so he could fix his car and drive himself home."

Grandmother nodded. "Well, I suppose no harm was done, though in the future, please remember that my house is not a youth hostel. Caspar is quite upset by Mr. Smith's presence."

"Okay," I said. After I dressed and ran Grandmother's daily bath (we kept a sturdy chair by the tub so she could get herself in and out of it) I went into the drawing room to wake Josh.

He was already up, sitting amid the tousled blankets, his eyes bleary, his shirt crumpled. Caspar sat on his lap, kneading his claws into Josh's leg. I could hear the cat's raspy purr all the way across the room. How could Grandmother misconstrue that kind of obvious contentment?

"Good morning," I said.

"Morning."

"I see Caspar found you."

"He curled up on my neck in the middle of the night. I thought I was going to suffocate. And then this morning, when I opened my eyes, he was staring at me."

"He likes you. Listen, Grandmother saw you in here and wanted to know why you'd spent the night on her couch. I couldn't tell her about the boat, for obvious reasons. It might be better if you were gone by the time she finishes getting dressed."

Josh pushed Caspar aside and pulled on his boots. "What did you tell her?"

"That your car broke down. That you were going to fix it this morning and drive yourself home."

We began folding blankets. "The truth, more or less. Change car to boat and—"

"Josh, are you going to tell her?"

He nodded slowly. "Yes. Now that I know what happened, I can't lie to her anymore."

"When are you going to tell her?"

"Tonight, after my lesson." He ran a finger down my cheek and added, "I'm so terribly sorry we involved you. When I explain it to her, I'll make her understand that you were duped into silence."

I nodded, knowing that he didn't understand how complicated he was going to make my life, knowing that simple explanations were not going to make much of an impact on Grandmother, yet reluctant to tell him. Now that he felt as though he was wrong, as though Gerald was wrong, the lie of his identity had ceased to be a forgivable act of kindness, and had turned instead into a devious charade. He had to get everything out in the open, and I cared about him too much to tell him where that was going to leave me, because then his hands would be tied.

Today would probably be the last day Grandmother would be able to stand the sight of me.

The day passed as slowly as a day spent anticipating a dentist appointment passes. I spent the morning at the shop. I even went ahead and bought the freshwater pearl necklace, planning to leave it in Grandmother's house. There was little doubt in my mind that she would demand my departure, and that posed another problem. I didn't have an apartment in Oakland to retreat to; it was still sublet to Jeanie's brother and would be for another six weeks.

"What's your problem today?" Bonnie asked as she switched the display of onyx and mother-of-pearl with the one of Southwestern turquoise.

I looked up from taping the paper on the necklace box. "I don't have a problem."

"Sure you do. You're usually so cheerful. Today you seem kind of preoccupied."

I shrugged.

"Your grandma?"

"Well, it's possible I might be kicked out of the house tonight for reasons entirely too complicated to go into, and since my home in Oakland is sublet, I really have nowhere to go."

"So come stay with me," she said casually as she placed an onyx watch against a clump of brain coral.

"Do you mean it?"

"Sure, why not? My place isn't fancy, but you're welcome to the sofa."

"Bonnie, I can't believe it. Thank you very much."

She shrugged her plump shoulders. "Listen, I don't want to lose you, not ever. If you have to leave at the end of summer, so be it, but I'll fight to keep you every day till then. I just told you so that you don't get to feeling like you owe me or anything."

"Okay," I said, and pinned a huge red bow on the necklace box, one gigantic worry off my mind.

I spent the afternoon shopping and cooking a few meals ahead of time, things that would need only defrosting and reheating. I also made a few calls and found an agency that would, for a price, send someone to the house once a day to check on Grandmother, give her a ride to the doctor's office or to a grocery store, and do light housekeeping chores. I told them I'd call them and arrange the details the next day, but that was another worry off my mind. I knew that after tonight, Grandmother wouldn't accept help from me, but with any luck she'd take a little help from an impersonal source. Maybe we could fix it so that she didn't even know it was coming from me.

By the time we both sat down to bowls of clam chowder and fresh sourdough bread, I was exhausted. Caspar lapped his soup from a bowl by Grandmother's feet, but it was all I could do to lift the spoon. I still had to pack my things and—

"Ellen, are you getting sick? You look awful."

"What? Oh, no, I'm fine. I didn't get a lot of sleep last night."

"Yes, and I've been meaning to talk to you about that too. I heard the door close at two-thirty this morning. Was that you?"

"Yes, I suppose that was me," I said with a deep sigh.

"With Mr. Smith?"

"You know he was with me."

She clicked her tongue three or four times. "It's quite true you're not a child, Ellen, but do you really feel that it's proper to bring a man you barely know into your home and have him stay the night after you spend the entire evening in his company?"

"Probably not proper at all," I agreed as I sipped my soup.

"And you're engaged. What would your fiancé think?"

I smiled. I mean, you had to love this woman. A few days before, she'd been trying to sell me on the idea of dating Tyrone Rathers because Danny didn't come visit, and now she was turning around and using Danny to convince me to mend my wicked ways with Josh. I looked at Grandmother, ready to tell her that Danny would probably think nothing of this, as nothing had happened, and probably wouldn't think anything of it even if something had happened, but I saw those blasted dark circles under her eyes again, and I remembered the bombshell Josh was going to drop in her lap in a few minutes, so I clamped my mouth shut and said nothing.

"Good, I can tell you are thinking about what I said." She picked up her mug, downed her soup, and asked for more. As I poured the soup, I heard the doorbell ring, and Grandmother said, "Never mind, Ellen. Mr. Smith is here."

If he was smart, I decided as I finished dinner, Josh would tell Grandmother the bad news before she gave him the lesson. She always liked him more before he actually played than she did after he'd tortured her for forty-five minutes. As I listened to him mutilate some perfectly innocent song most eight-year-olds with a few weeks' worth of piano lessons under their belts could master, I decided that maybe he wasn't as smart as he looked. Or maybe he was putting off the unpleasant chore ahead.

I washed dishes, packed an overnight bag, checked the phone book for Bonnie's home address, and sat on the edge of the bed. Caspar came into my room and sat with me, conspicuously not purring. He either could sense my nerves or hated Josh's piano playing.

At last, the ''music'' stopped. A few minutes later, Grandmother called my name and I went into the piano room.

''Over here,'' she called from the drawing room. ''Mr. Smith brought me a bottle of my favorite sherry. Join us, won't you, Ellen?''

I looked at Josh as I crossed the rug and decided he looked as nervous as I felt. He handed me a tiny glass of sherry, which I took even though I don't like the stuff, and we both sat on the sofa. Grandmother was already seated in her favorite chair. Caspar appeared, leaped onto the chair's back, and promptly fell asleep. The room was suffocatingly warm, as it was a mild summer evening, but the fire was roaring on the grate as usual.

The scene was set, all cozy and welcoming.

Josh cleared his throat. He said, ''I want to tell you something, Mrs. Brookfield.''

She leaned slightly forward. I noticed a dab of clam

chowder had left a pale yellow stain on her white sling. ''What is it, Mr. Smith?''

He cleared his throat again. ''Well, I want you to know that I realize I'm not very good on the piano yet, but I really do enjoy these lessons.''

''That's nice,'' she said, adding uncertainly, ''I'm sure, in time, you'll improve.''

''I hope so.'' He gulped down the sherry and then he stared at me. I handed him my untouched glass, which he gulped down as well (earning a frown from Grandmother). He took a deep breath and said, ''First, I want to say that I'm sorry I deceived you. I had no right, but please believe me that at the time, I didn't realize what had really happened.''

''You're speaking in riddles, Mr. Smith,'' Grandmother cautioned.

''Yes, I am. Well, Mrs. Brookfield, the truth of the matter is that I'm not really Josh Smith. My name is Josh Holt. I'm Gerald Holt's grandson.''

Grandmother set the glass of sherry down so hard some of the liquid spilled over the lip. She stared at Josh, her complexion draining of color the way it had the first time I'd told her about Gerald Holt.

''His grandson,'' she whispered.

He nodded. ''Yes, ma'am. I want you to know that when I agreed to come here and try to get you to see Granddad, I had no idea what had really happened. I didn't understand. If I had—''

"And you've known all along, haven't you?" she asked, turning her attention to me, her blue eyes blazing with repressed fury. "Of course you knew," she answered for me. "And yet you told me nothing!"

"It wasn't like that," Josh said. "She didn't understand, either. Let me explain—"

"No!" Grandmother rose to her feet in one fluid motion. She looked at Josh again and said, "You get out of my home, right now. And don't come back here, not ever again, do you understand?"

Josh swallowed back whatever else he wanted to say. There was no getting around the fact that Grandmother had a right to the last word, and even if she was going to call the game early, her wishes had to be respected.

"Where are you going?" she asked me as I stood.

"I'm going to a friend's house," I said.

"No, you're not."

"Yes, Grandmother, I am. I'm terribly sorry about what's happened here. I can imagine how betrayed you feel, and since I was part of it, I think it would be best if I left. I've made certain arrangements, but really, you're not handicapped by this broken arm—"

"You can imagine how betrayed I feel?" she interrupted. "You can imagine what it feels like to be stood up at the altar by the only man you've ever loved? You can imagine the looks, the way people whispered behind your back, the hurried marriage to a man twenty years your senior because in your father's eye you were damaged goods! No, young lady, I don't think you can imagine it at all.''

''Well, maybe not, but—''

''And now, fifty-five years later, I take a young man into my home as a student, I trust him, I—I . . . like him, and then he betrays me too. Of course he's Gerald Holt's grandson! Who else could be so hateful?''

''Grandmother—''

''But you, Ellen. My own granddaughter. Sneaking around behind my back, lying to me, laughing at me! How could you? How *could* you?''

She clutched her bad arm, and I saw tears sliding down her cheeks. My heart ached for her. She hated scenes, and yet here she was, at the center of a doozy. I looked at Josh and said, ''You'd better go. Call me in a couple of days. Better call at the shop, because I don't know where I'll be.''

''You can't stay here,'' he said. ''Not now.''

''I know.''

Grandmother, as white as her cat, shook her head. Then she quietly fainted.

Chapter Eleven

By the time Grandmother came to, Josh had carried her into her room, kissed me on the top of my head as I called the doctor, and promised to call me at exactly eight o'clock the next morning. "I shouldn't have told her," he said. "It only made things worse."

There was no arguing that fact, not with Grandmother out like a light. I'd known all along that she'd be upset, but it had never occurred to me that she'd actually faint! I squeezed Josh's hand and closed the door behind him.

Grandmother regained consciousness as Dr. Pullman hurried into her room, with me trailing along behind.

"Get that cat off the bed," he said immediately.

Caspar got the hint all on his own and jumped down from the foot of the bed, where he'd curled into a ball beside Grandmother's feet.

"Naomi, are you all right?"

"Of course I'm not all right," she mumbled.

I backed out of the way, sure that the sight of my face would send her into another dead faint. Dr. Pullman stuck a thermometer into her mouth while he took her blood pressure and listened to her heart.

"Blood pressure is okay," he said. He turned around and looked at me. "What happened?"

I explained, sort of. I said she'd had an emotionally charged scene, then fainted. The doctor shook his head. "Did she fall on that arm?"

"No, I'm certain she didn't. In fact, she kind of landed on the chair."

"Then how did she get in here?" He looked at me, as though assessing my ability to haul my grandmother between rooms, and added, "You?"

"No. A friend—"

"Not a friend!" she snapped. She handed the doctor his thermometer. "Not a friend," she repeated miserably.

"Didn't I tell you to keep her well rested?" he asked me. "Didn't I tell you to see to it that she cut down on her lessons and took a nap every afternoon? Is she doing that?"

"Well, not exactly—"

"It is your responsibility, young woman, to see to it that she does."

He didn't understand, and I didn't know how to explain with Grandmother hanging on our every word.

"Poppycock!" she said.

The doctor had his fingers on her wrist, taking her pulse. "What did you say?" he demanded.

"You heard me. This girl does not run my life. I do that."

"And you do it so well that I'm tempted to slap you in a nursing home for a couple of months."

"You'll do nothing of the sort!"

"I will if you don't stay in this bed for a week."

They glared at each other. Finally, Grandmother said, "Okay. I will stay in bed for a week."

You could have knocked me over with a feather.

"Good. And you will do what Ellen tells you to do?"

"She won't want me—" I started to say.

"Yes," Grandmother interrupted. "I will do what she tells me to do."

The doctor nodded. "All right, then. But we'll have to X-ray that arm tomorrow morning first thing, just to make sure you didn't whack it when you fainted." He turned to me. "You'll bring her into the office, first thing?"

"Yes, okay." Suddenly I felt weary beyond words.

"You must keep her calm," Dr. Pullman said as I

walked him to the door. "People don't faint for no reason. I've sedated her for tonight, and I'll have some pills for her tomorrow when you come in, but for now, see to it that nothing or no one upsets her."

"I'll try," I told him.

"Her very life may be in your hands," he said ominously before I locked the door behind him, dreading the moment when I'd have to go back into Grandmother's room.

"Ellen?" she called as I closed the fire grate and drew the curtains.

There was nothing to do but attend to her wishes. "What is it?" I asked from her doorway.

She patted the bed next to her, a gesture at once so homey and so foreign to her nature that she had to do it twice before I really believed she wanted me to come. I sat down facing her; Caspar was between us, like a fluffy white neutral zone.

"I've decided not to blame you," she said, her voice slurred with fatigue. "I know how deceitful Holt men can be. I know how they can promise things and then walk away. I know how they can use a woman."

"Josh isn't like that," I protested.

She shook her head impatiently. "Of course he is. He proved that tonight, didn't he?"

"Let's not talk about Josh," I said. "You must be drowsy. Go to sleep—"

"You have your fiancé," she said as her eyes closed. "We must see that you marry him soon."

"Yes, yes," I said soothingly, patting her hand. When I was sure she was asleep, I turned off the lamp and left the room, leaving the door open in case she called out in the night.

"Oh, what a tangled web we weave . . ." the saying goes. What was the next part? Something like, "When first we practice to deceive." The poet who wrote those lines had obviously had me in mind. The thing was, the whole affair was really kind of stupid. Grandmother liked Josh; he liked her. I suspected I was falling in love with him, and I now kind of liked my grandmother for the first time in my life. I liked Gerald, even though he'd done a really rotten thing in the past and he was torturing himself over a mistake fifty-five years old. Grandmother, of course, was full of virtuous outrage, revenge running hot in her veins.

What was the point of hanging on to all that bitterness all this time?

I couldn't even sit her down and talk to her about it. I couldn't risk hurting her, and the doctor had made it quite clear that this could happen. But if I let things slide along the way they were, nothing would be resolved, and if my future did happen to be linked with Josh's future, how would we avoid a confrontation? Josh owned an island—he wasn't going to be leaving Eureka. Grandmother wasn't going anywhere, either.

Was there going to be some point down the road where she could handle more stress? It seemed unlikely.

I spent a fitful night on the sofa, and dragged around the house from four A.M. on. Grandmother was still sleeping at eight when the phone rang. I picked it up before the first ring was finished.

"Ellen? How is she?"

"She's okay. The doctor wants to X-ray her arm to make sure it wasn't hurt when she fell."

"I'm sure it wasn't. She kind of just sat back in the chair."

"That's what I thought. The worst part—for me, that is—is that I'm now responsible for making sure nothing bothers her. I am not to do or say anything that might cause her one moment's distress."

"Which means you aren't going to be seeing me at her house."

"I can't even leave here for a week," I said. "She's agreed to spend a week in bed."

"A week." The time sentence stretched between us like a desert before a weary traveler. "It's going to be a long seven days," he added. "Ellen, I'm going to say it one more time. I'm sorry. That was the last apology I'm ever going to make to you. From now on, I'm going to have to be perfect."

"That's a tall order, Josh. How is Gerald?"

"Hard to tell. I told him about the scene last night. I thought it was important that he understand once and for all that Naomi Brookfield would be happiest if Gerald Holt left her alone forever. He was upset to hear she fainted, but this morning, he's actually up and dressed and gone already. He seems to have accepted it and decided to get on with his life.''

"That's good.''

"Let's hope it lasts. I'll call you tomorrow, okay? Maybe a little later, as Brennan wants to come look at his boat before he goes to work.''

"Okay. Is the boat done?''

"Everything but her try-out sail. I was hoping you could come along for that.''

"When are you going?''

"Sunday afternoon.''

"I don't see how I can, but maybe something will turn up. Don't write me off completely.''

"No chance. Well, sweetheart, take care of yourself and Mrs. Brookfield.''

"I will.'' I felt all toasty inside, the way you do when someone you love calls you a pet name. My "real life" had been snatched away once this summer already; I'd replaced it with another, one that suddenly seemed superior to the old one, and now that was receding as well. With a sigh, I picked up the phone and called Bonnie to tell her I wouldn't be in for at least a week.

* * *

What Grandmother and I both forgot about was her piano students! We went to the doctor, got the X ray and the new pills, stopped off at the market because she had a craving for fresh strawberries, and drove home. And there, sitting on the stoop, was Kelly Wooster, eight years old, second-year student. She smiled at us as I unlocked the door.

"You'll have to go home," I said.

Grandmother stiffened. "No. Kelly, go sit on the piano bench. I'll be there in a moment."

I shook my head. "You promised," I reminded Grandmother as I closed the music-room doors.

"I know, but I told you this before, Ellen. I can't afford to give up my students."

"I have money—"

"I will not accept money from you!" she said. She looked older today, tired and worn out. I kept hearing Dr. Pullman cautioning me to watch out for her. Maybe she was as frail as he seemed to think she was.

"You're in no shape to teach a lesson," I said gently. "You must go to bed, and that's all there is to it."

"Then *you* teach the lesson."

"Me?"

"You've studied for years."

"A long time ago. I don't remember any of it."

"Hogwash! You teach it or I will."

I could feel panic stampeding through my body,

urging me to open the front door and run back to Oakland. Ah, responsibility, that awful curse that slams doors as fast as imagination opens them! Of course I couldn't go, but how I longed to!

"I can't," I said again. "I was an awful student—"

"You were an exceptional student."

Now the world was topsy-turvy. "You always told me how sloppy I was and how—"

"To get you to work harder," she said.

I felt my fingernails bite into my palms as I clenched my fists. "You never once told me a positive thing. Because of you, I hated the piano."

Grandmother almost swooned. I'd reverted to being twelve years old—I'd forgotten who was the vulnerable one now. I grabbed her good arm and steadied her. "Go to bed," I said. "I'll teach Kelly's lesson."

"And then Todd Bracken and Jason Orick?"

"Yes, yes, whatever you want. As long as you rest."

"I *am* tired," she admitted, and she let me settle her on her bed with a warm blanket pulled up to her chin.

Kelly tackled the keys with childlike abandon, ripping through the different songs with more enthusiasm than perfection.

"Aren't you going to set the tick-tock machine?" she asked.

"The tick-tock—you mean the metronome? No, I'm not going to set it."

"Mrs. Brookfield always sets it," the child said.

So, I set it. It didn't seem to make the slightest difference in her poor timing, but she appeared content and I'd only signed on for a week.

After Kelly came Todd, and after Todd came Jason. I did what I could to direct their small fingers, but when Jason asked me to play a particular passage to show him how it was supposed to sound, I fumbled more than he did. Of course, he loved this and laughed till his face was red.

After Jason left, I heated the leftover chowder and took a mug and a few crackers in to Grandmother. I propped her up with a half-dozen pillows, then set the tray across her lap.

"I heard the piano," she told me.

"All three lessons went fine," I assured her cheerfully. If I was going to be drafted into head nurse, then I would darn well be a positive one.

"Tyrone comes this afternoon. So does Mary Jade and Felix Williams."

"They're advanced students," I said. "They'll resent having a novice teacher. I'd better call and cancel their lessons."

Grandmother took a sip of soup. "You're forgetting that the recital is Sunday."

The recital. She was right, I had forgotten.

"You'll have to go and represent me. The advanced students can play here today; it's their last opportunity before the recital. Just leave the doors open, and I'll listen. I can make notes by speaking into my little tape recorder. After their lessons, send each of them in and I'll go over their pieces individually. Now, Ellen, what fault can you find in this plan?"

"Just that it means you won't be able to sleep."

"I slept all morning, and I assume I'll sleep all night. Surely you and that quack Pullman can't object to my having three alert hours in the middle of the day!" Her eyes were blazing, her cheeks were pink.

"Whatever you want," I said. "What time is the recital?"

"Ten o'clock Sunday. You will go for me, won't you, Ellen?"

As if I had a choice. "If I can find someone to come stay with you, I will."

She nodded, lying back on her pillows. "You will. You're very good at arranging little things like that."

The afternoon passed more quickly than I thought it would. At least the advanced students knew how to play without hurting the listener, and their selections were polished because of the impending recital. They were all deferential to me because I was related to their Mrs. Brookfield; therefore, I must play like a whiz. I said nothing to disabuse them of this silly notion, but I was smart enough never to touch the keys.

I fixed dinner as Grandmother went over the last lesson with Felix Williams, a nice boy of about fourteen with ten zillion freckles. Caspar took up camp by my feet in case a shrimp should fall into his waiting mouth. When I heard the front door close, I went into Grandmother's bedroom with a glass of juice and another pill.

"How are you doing?" I asked.

"Felix's timing was all wrong. I hope he practices before Sunday. You know, Ellen, it sometimes seems to me that the students nowadays aren't as dedicated as their parents were."

"Did you compliment Felix at all?" I asked. He'd played Rachmaninoff's Prelude in C# Minor with all the gusto the piece requires. I'd been quite impressed with his rendition.

"Compliment him? Did you hear the way he fumbled the last three bars? He's going to have to sharpen his work if he expects to do well at the recital."

I sat down. "Isn't a recital just that, Grandmother— a recital? I mean, it isn't a contest, is it?"

"Everything is a contest," she snapped. "A person must never be content with mediocrity." She handed me the empty glass and added, "What's for dinner?"

"Scampi."

"Will you bring me the red piano book in the bench?

I'll read it while you cook. Are you boiling pasta to go with the shrimp?''

"I'm making rice.''

"I would prefer linguine. The red book, Ellen.''

I dutifully got her the red book; then I dug through the cupboard for linguine and put the cooked rice in the refrigerator for another day.

When the doorbell rang, I expected to find Dr. Pullman checking up on my bedside manner. What I found was a florist deluged with flowers.

"Mimi?'' he asked.

"Oh, no, not again.''

"What?''

"Who are these from?'' I asked, as if I didn't know.

"No name. I guess they're anonymous.''

The young man was holding two arrangements, one of tiny pink roses, the other of blue irises. They were absolutely exquisite. "Take them back,'' I said.

"I can't do that,'' he protested.

"Then take them to a hospital or something.''

"All of them?''

"You mean there's more?''

He handed me the roses and the irises, and went back to his van. When he climbed the front steps again, he was holding yellow tulips and white calla lilies. "There's more,'' he said. By the time he was finished, over twenty different arrangements or bouquets were piled on the doorstep and in the drawing room.

"Cleaned out the shop," the delivery boy said. I gave him a couple of dollars and stood looking at all the flowers, wondering what I was supposed to do with them.

"What's this?" Grandmother asked from the kitchen. She approached the flowers warily, as though they were enemies.

I said, "Anonymous flowers."

"From *him?*"

"I think so."

"Put them outside," she said with a controlled wave of her hand.

I started through to the back door, but she called me back. "No, put them out the front door. If he's lurking around, I want him to see that his honor can't be reclaimed with a few flowers."

I piled all the flowers on the front porch. They were so beautiful and so fragrant that it broke my heart to waste them. I looked up and down the street, wondering if Gerald was watching, wondering how deep a pit of depression this act of rejection would send him into. The man sure didn't know how to take a hint!

After dinner, while Grandmother read a book in her bed, Caspar and I sat on the back steps. I could hear the neighbors barbecuing and was shocked at the jealousy I felt upon hearing normal people leading normal lives. The man was telling the woman that she was going to burn his steak the way she did every time, so she told him to do it himself, and they both laughed as though this was some long-standing joke between them.

My time as Grandmother's nurse was limited. Within a few weeks, I would be returning to Oakland, though I suspected that because of Josh I'd be making frequent trips north. Even if Grandmother were restricted to bed for the rest of the year, my job would be over when Mom came home. I missed Josh and yearned to see him, but I would live for a while, and so would he.

But what about Grandmother? Where were her friends? Who did she see besides the children and young adults who came to the house for lessons, and a few other piano teachers at the infrequent recitals? Most of her friends were either housebound or gone. She lived in a small neighborhood, but she didn't know her neighbors.

I had the sudden urge to march to the fence and introduce myself, and before I could think of a half-dozen reasons why I shouldn't, I did just that.

The wooden fence was about six feet tall, too high for me actually to see over, but there was a crosspiece wide enough to put a foot on about a foot from the ground. I stood on this piece of wood and peered into the neighbors' backyard.

Unlike Grandmother's yard, which had been well thought out at some distant time in the past but which now suffered from neglect, the neighbors' yard was picture perfect. The perimeter was decorated with evergreen shrubs, flowering bushes made accent points of color, and a small vegetable/flower garden ringed a little concrete patio. A big round barbecue sat in the center of the patio, and two steaks sizzled on the grill. A man and a woman were sitting on lawn chairs, he sipping beer from the can, she flipping through a magazine. They noticed me staring at them immediately.

"Sorry to intrude," I said. "I just wanted to say hello."

The woman got up from her chair. She was an attractive blonde about my age with a pert nose, curly hair, and an obviously distended middle covered by a navy-and-white–striped maternity top. "Were you related to the old lady?" she asked.

Were? "I'm her granddaughter," I said.

She looked at her husband. "See, Mark, I told you they were related." She looked back at me and explained. "We saw you going into the house sometime last month, and I told Mark you must be related because you kind of look like her. Listen, we didn't know her, but we're real sorry, aren't we, Mark?"

Mark said, "Yes. If there's anything we can do, please let us know." He was a big man with a sturdy, no-nonsense look about him.

"I'm afraid I don't understand," I protested.

"About your grandma's death," she explained.

"My grandmother isn't dead," I said.

The woman looked at her husband, then back at me. "I saw all the flowers on the porch, and I assumed. . . ." She stopped talking because I was laughing into my hand.

"I'm sorry," I said, catching my breath. "Those were sent by a secret admirer—well, sort of. Anyway, she didn't want them in the house, so we piled them outside."

The man slapped his bare leg as he hooted laughter. "There you go again, Dawn, making assumptions."

She smiled. "Well, I'm just glad I was wrong."

"Me too. By the way, my name is Ellen Nickleson."

"Dawn Fulkerson, and that's Mark. Honey, my steak is burning."

Mark jumped up from his chair. He waved at me and said hello, but his mind was clearly back on dinner.

"I'll let you go," I said. "I just wanted to meet you."

"I'm glad you did. I'll be truthful with you. I tried being friendly with your grandmother when we first moved into the house, but she was kind of standoffish, so I gave up." She wrinkled her nose and added, "Does she teach music or something?"

"Piano."

"I thought so. Listen, you come over and visit me sometime. Must be kind of dreadful being stuck in that house day after day."

"It hasn't been bad. She has a broken arm. That's why I'm here."

"She does? I didn't know that."

"Honey, your dinner is ready," Mark said. He looked at me and added politely, "Would you care to join us?"

"I already ate, but thanks." With a nod and a wave, I left them to eat their dinner in peace, content in each other's company. By the look of Dawn's midsection, they wouldn't be eating too many more meals alone.

"Who were you talking to?" Grandmother asked when I went back inside.

"Your neighbors, Dawn and Mark Fulkerson." I longed to tell her how they'd thought she'd died and the flowers outside were from the funeral. Of course, I didn't. "They're very nice. She's going to have a baby."

"Great," Grandmother scoffed. "All I need is a squawking baby to keep me awake nights."

"If she can put up with the piano lessons you give, it seems to me that you can put up with a baby," I said matter-of-factly.

I sneaked a look to see how she was taking this suggestion and found her yawning. "Maybe it's time for you to hit the sack," I said.

"That's all I've done all day. Don't know why I'm so sleepy. Remember that you have a piano lesson at nine o'clock sharp tomorrow morning. Emily Perkins.''

''I'll remember.''

''You aren't going out?'' she asked.

''No, I'm not going out.''

''Because Josh Holt is as deceitful as his grandfather was.'' She yawned while she said this, and it occurred to me that it was so much rhetoric by now, words she said but hardly listened to.

''Go to sleep.'' I barely made it to the door before she began snoring.

The evening passed like a snail. Caspar wasn't exactly stimulating company, there was nothing interesting on television, and my mind wandered too much to read. I would have given my right foot to see Josh's face at the door. Was it really possible we'd made that silly trek through town from the old boat harbor only forty-eight hours before? It seemed like two lifetimes.

I went out on the front porch and sat amid the flowers. One arrangement was loaded with daisies, so I spent time pulling petals, saying, ''He loves me/he loves me not'' over and over until even that grew old. I plucked pink roses from a vase and carried them inside, where I put them on my nightstand. Which put me face-to-face—in a manner of speaking—with Danny Gorman.

Where was he? I'd been trying to call for the better

part of two days, and still he didn't answer his phone. What would I say to him if he did answer?

I've fallen in love with someone else, I decided I would say, because that's exactly what had happened. And even if it didn't work out with Josh for some reason, at least now I knew what love was, now I knew what to search for.

But it had to work out with Josh, I thought immediately, suspecting that without Josh, life wasn't really worth the effort.

Chapter Twelve

I wasn't going to say it, but my mind repeated, *One-two, one-two,* over and over as Emily Perkins's little fingers fumbled on the notes of a song grandly called "Piano Melody."

"Very good," I said, and she spared me a gap-toothed smile.

"I'm playing in the recital," she informed me. "Mommy is making Daddy come."

"How nice." I suppressed a grin. "Try the song again, Emily, and this time, try to hit all the lower keys, okay? And try not to make the upper keys so much louder than the lower keys."

As I listened to her I listened for the phone. Grandmother had asked me to bring it into her room for the morning, as she had some calls to make. I'd told her I was expecting a personal call and to please holler for me, but so far, I hadn't heard a word. I glanced at my watch. It was only nine forty-five. Josh was probably still showing Mr. Brennan his new boat.

"Was that better?" Emily asked.

I nodded, even though I hadn't heard a single note. "Be sure to be at the Gold Lion Hotel at ten A.M.," I reminded her. "Don't be late."

"I won't." She gathered up her books and skipped to the front door.

"Would you like some flowers?" I asked.

Her eyes grew wide. "Really?"

"Really. How about some daffodils?"

She accepted the flowers. Her mother was in the car, and I could see her watch Emily approach with the wild mass of bright yellow flowers, her eyes as wide as her daughter's. I closed the front door and made my way back to Grandmother's bedroom.

"Need anything before the next lesson?" I asked.

She shook her head. She was propped on the pillows again, a notebook open before her, a pencil between her teeth. She took the pencil out and asked, "Jenny Bachman is next?"

"Yes. You said this morning that she's a fourth-year student."

"She's a good student, but don't make a fuss over her. It'll ruin her concentration."

"I'll rap her over the knuckles with a ruler," I said. "I'm just kidding, Grandmother."

She narrowed her eyes, clearly telling me music was nothing to kid about. "Did I get a call yet?" I asked.

"No, you didn't get a call. I think I hear the doorbell."

Sure enough, the doorbell rang. "You're supposed to be napping," I reminded her as I hurried off to welcome Jenny Bachman.

Jenny's playing was good and I did compliment her; she deserved it. I'm afraid I wasn't terribly attentive, as half of me was waiting for the phone to ring and half of me was afraid of what Grandmother would say when it did and she heard Josh's voice. But it didn't ring, and pretty soon Jenny left (with a vase of red rosebuds) and Harold Myer arrived, and then he left (blue irises) and it was time to make lunch.

Grandmother ate hers in bed. I took the phone out to the kitchen and tried calling Josh, but he didn't answer. "Are you sure no one called?" I asked one last time.

"Just that Holt boy," she said as she bit into a juicy strawberry.

"Josh? What did he want, Grandmother?"

She consulted her notebook. "He left you a message, that's all."

I swallowed my impatience. "What was the message?"

"He said that he didn't want to see you for a while, that he'd talk to you in a couple of weeks, if you were still here."

I tried to keep my face from reflecting the devastation I felt in my heart. "He said that?" I asked.

She shrugged. "I tried to warn you, Ellen. Now, Peter Dunn comes this afternoon. I'll make him a tape the way I did for the others, so remember to keep the doors open. Are there more berries?"

I sank down onto a chair. Why would Josh say something like that? I looked askance at my grand-mother. Would she lie to me about Josh?

"Ellen, try not to look so stricken. I'd like to remind you that you're engaged."

I didn't dare move, fearing that my legs would fail to support me. The air in the room seemed tight. I knew my eyes were bright with unshed tears. All I wanted was to be whisked away to some private place where I could suffer without an audience.

"Maybe now you have a slight taste of what Gerald Holt put me through fifty-five years ago," she said suddenly.

I sprang to my feet and ran from the room.

Somehow I made it through Peter's lesson and then two more lessons. Toward dinnertime, a knock on the door sent my heart pounding, and I ran to answer it.

"Hi!" Dawn Fulkerson said. "I brought your grandmother some chocolate cake. Chocolate always makes me feel better. How about you?''

I thought I could eat my way through Hershey, Pennsylvania, and it wouldn't help a bit. I said, ''It was very kind of you.''

''I thought it was time I got to know her. Thinking she was dead yesterday, well, it got me to thinking about how I'd feel if she really did die and I'd never made an effort to be friendly.''

''She's in here.'' I led Dawn into Grandmother's room. To my surprise and relief, Grandmother was polite and as charming as she can be when it behooves her to be polite and charming. What would this woman have been like if Gerald Holt had married her?

''Well, I won't stay. I know how it is when you don't feel well and strangers talk and talk,'' Dawn said after a while.

''It was very kind of you to bring the cake,'' Grandmother told her. ''I hope now that we've met, you'll be coming back.''

''Really? Sure, I'd like that. And maybe someday you can give little Junior here piano lessons!''

Grandmother laughed!

I saw Dawn to the door the way any well-trained maid does, insisted she take three flower arrangements home with her (that was all she could carry), and was about to close the door when I saw a car pull up to the curb and a man in a black tux get out. He was carrying a violin case. He walked up to the door, looked at the flowers, and asked, "Is this the residence of Mimi Brookfield?"

"Oh, dear," I said.

He was a tall man with a long thin nose and a way of looking down it that intimidated me. He said, "I beg your pardon, madam. Are you or are you not Mimi Brookfield?"

"I am not," I told him.

"Then would you be so kind as to take me to her?"

The doctor had said, *Keep her quiet and rested. No surprises, no upsets.*

I said, "Follow me," deciding on the spot to ignore the doctor's orders.

"Grandmother," I announced, "you have another visitor."

The man made an entrance. He had the violin out of the case and was playing it by the time he stepped into her room. I don't know what he played, but he played it exceptionally well. I saw tears gather in Grandmother's eyes and I wiped a few from my own.

He played three selections, each one more romantic and haunting than the one before. I had wondered how Grandmother would go about throwing an imposing stranger out of her bedroom, but she acted as though she enjoyed his playing, even clapping one hand against her notebook when he finished the last selection.

"Bravo, bravo!" she said.

He bowed stiffly.

"Ellen, please get my purse."

The man touched my arm. "There is no need. I received a letter with this address and time, the names of these songs, and a hefty check. The check was from someone named Gerald Holt."

"Yes," Grandmother said, her voice kind of sad instead of angry. "Thank you," she added. "Ellen, after you show this gentleman out, would you please come back?"

So I pressed a few flowers on the violin player and went back into Grandmother's room. "He's sure persistent," I said. "And you have to admit he's not cheap."

She nodded. "Tomorrow evening, if something or someone comes, will you please stop it at the door?"

"Are you sure?" I asked, sensing a weakening.

"Most certain. Now, what's for dinner?"

I called Josh late at night, after Grandmother was asleep. It took forever for him to answer the phone, and though his voice was groggy when he said hello, it cleared immediately when he heard my voice.

"Ellen?"

"Josh, I'm sorry I woke you."

"It's okay, sweet—" He stopped the endearment

abruptly and began again. "What's wrong? It's two
A.M. Are you okay? Is Mrs. Brookfield okay?"

"We're fine," I assured him. When he'd cut short
saying *sweetheart* it had answered several questions
for me, and now I didn't know what I wanted.

"Things were happening too fast," he said out of
the blue.

"That's true," I agreed, afraid to tell him how I
really felt, afraid to blurt out *I love you, I love you* the
way I wanted to.

"Maybe in a few weeks, after we've had some
space. . . ."

"Yeah. Well, sorry I woke you up."

"It's okay," he repeated, and darned if he didn't
sound as close to tears as I was.

On Friday, as the clock ticked down to five, I waited
in the drawing room, curious about what would happen
tonight. Grandmother was waiting in her room, Caspar
by her side, and I knew she was as nervous about it
as I was.

Five came and went, and I was just beginning to
think Gerald had finally given up, when Grandmother
yelled my name. I ran back to her room and stopped
short in the doorway.

Her window was open because it was so warm outside, and the curtains fluttered in the breeze. Through

the window wafted the distinctive sound of a Mexican mariachi band.

"I told you to stop them at the door," she hissed.

"They didn't come to the door. Look at them, Grandmother—they have beautiful costumes."

I helped her out of bed and drew a chair up to the window where she sat in her nightgown, her hair tidy and neat as always, two bright color spots in her cheeks.

She listened attentively for thirty-five minutes as they sang to her in a language she couldn't understand but which clearly spoke of love. One guitar player, handsome with a dashing mustache and a black velvet hat, threw her a red rosebud, which she fielded with her one good hand.

"Gerald sure is inventive," I observed.

Grandmother nodded. "He's wasting his money," she said. "I think I'll take a bath."

The next day was Saturday, which in and of itself was hardly noteworthy, but because it was the second day of my life without Josh, a day without lessons, the day before the recital, and one month to the day before I would drive back to Oakland to reclaim my old life, I suppose it deserved a certain importance. Still, it was all I could do to drag through it.

I spent hours going over Grandmother's notes with her. She was frantic lest something go wrong during the recital, and no matter how many times I assured her that things were bound to go smoothly, she fussed and fumed. I just couldn't understand what all the hoopla was about. After all, the only audience would be composed of family members and close friends— one would be hard pressed to come across a more generous crowd.

But Grandmother saw it differently. To her, this was like a giant advertisement. When the advanced students played, she wanted the parents of younger students to see what their child could turn into. When the younger children played, she wanted the parents of students of different teachers to say to themselves, "Hmm— maybe my little Jane or Johnny should be studying music with Naomi Brookfield!"

As five o'clock rolled around, I noticed Grandmother's eyes straying more and more frequently to the clock. I felt my own stomach tighten into a knot. Not knowing what to expect, Grandmother had insisted on getting dressed, and she sat in the drawing room, ramrod straight in her chair, Caspar curled up on her lap. She was wearing her best blue blouse and had cajoled me into tying her prettiest scarf as a sling. "I'm not going to be caught in my robe again," she'd said as I helped her fix her hair.

And now the clock ticked as slowly as it used to when I sat before the piano, my palms sweaty, my heart racing. What if Gerald had given up? What if he didn't do anything?

And then we heard a racket out on the street. Grandmother peered through the window and said, "Oh, my gosh, Ellen. Open the front door, quick!"

So I opened the front door, and the racket turned into three drums beating out a rhythm at the rear of a high-school marching band. As soon as Grandmother stepped out onto the porch, the brass section struck up and began playing the Beatles tune "I Want to Hold Your Hand." As I dragged a chair out onto the porch and gently pushed Grandmother down onto it, the band marched up and down the street, going through snappy renditions of several more Beatles songs. I saw tears streaming down Grandmother's cheeks, and I hoped Dr. Pullman wouldn't choose this moment to stop by— he'd have a coronary! But medicine doesn't always come in a bottle, and tears are not always harmful. I had a feeling this was medicine for the soul and was going to do Grandmother a lot more good than those little white pills Dr. Pullman prescribed.

The Fulkersons appeared on their front porch, and Grandmother waved merrily at them. I saw other neighbors too, and except for one grouch who shouted something about the police, they all clapped and hollered after every number as the kids in the band—all thirty-two of them—began playing a simple melody I recognized, "The Most Beautiful Girl in the World."

As they played this last piece, they lined up on either side of the street. A truck with a flatbed appeared at the head of the block. The small crowd of onlookers moved aside to let the truck through until it stopped in front of Grandmother's house.

On the flatbed was a white baby-grand piano and a man in a white tuxedo. I hardly recognized Gerald Holt as he got up from the piano bench and bowed to Grandmother. The neighbors all cheered, and then everything became very quiet.

There were amplifiers on the flatbed truck. Gerald produced a microphone. He held it to his lips, his eyes glued to Grandmother's face. He cleared his throat, and then he said, "All this is for Mimi Brookfield, the most beautiful girl in the world. This is an apology, Mimi, and a question too: Will you forgive me?"

And then, without waiting for an answer, he sat back on the piano bench, poised his hands over the keyboard, and began picking out—one-fingered—"Heart and Soul." That was simple enough, but then he began to sing the words:

" 'Heart and soul, I fell in love with you,' " he crooned. His voice was a cross between fingernails scratching a blackboard and a wounded gull shrieking.

I looked at Grandmother and found her smiling. "He's making a fool of himself," she said, her voice pleased.

Two band members detached themselves from the

others and walked up to the porch. The young man held out his hand. Behind him, another band member was putting a carpeted flight of steps up to the bed of the truck. The intent was clear to me and everyone else. Gerald was asking her to join him. She could refuse him now, send him away embarrassed, and partially revenge her own humiliation.

As I held my breath, Grandmother stood and took the young man's hand. He helped her down the steps, across the street, and then up to the bed of the truck, where Gerald took her arm. No one else realized what was happening when they stood looking at each other. Everyone else saw two old people and a piano. They saw a man pinning a gaudy corsage onto a woman's blouse, tentative smiles, and two hands that shyly met for a second.

I saw the bandaging of a fifty-five-year-old wound, the reclaiming of pride and honor, the release of spite and revenge, and I suddenly found myself sitting on the chair, too overwhelmed to move.

The neighborhood would long talk about the way Grandmother sat on the piano bench and started tapping out the left hand of the "Heart and Soul" duet while Gerald stood behind her and fumbled with the right. After a few minutes, the band struck up the melody, and then they marched away. I would never find out how Gerald got the band to help him out—in the middle of the summer too. Tears in my eyes, I went into the house.

Eventually, Grandma and Gerald climbed down from the truck and came into the house too. Grandmother stopped before me, and her shaking fingers touched the corsage. Nestled in between two white orchids was the tiny gold piano and faded burgundy ribbon, saved by Gerald for fifty-five years for what other purpose than their eventual return to Grandmother? I looked at her face and said, "It's like a circle, isn't it?"

"Like a circle," she repeated. I felt tears gather in my eyes, and I blinked them away. I told myself they were tears of happiness for Gerald and Grandmother, but in my heart I knew: Those tears were for me too. For me and Josh and what we'd lost.

Grandmother took a deep breath as though plowing through a field of sentimentality. She looked away from me, back at Gerald. "Come into the drawing room," she said, and he closed the doors after them. I heard their raised voices for a half hour as they worked out their differences.

And then it got very quiet, and Caspar and I went back on the front porch.

Dawn was sitting outside too. She waved and hollered, "That was really something. Is he your Grandma's boyfriend?"

How to answer that one? "I don't know," I said truthfully.

"Well, I just hope that when we get to be her age, our men will still make a fuss over us like that, don't you?"

I'd settle for now, I wanted to say as I nodded non-committally. I'd settle for a year with Josh now. I didn't want to wait a lifetime. What was he afraid of, anyway? Had I been too pushy? I tried to think of what I'd said or done that could have scared him off, and I couldn't think of a thing.

Then, what?

A short honk brought me back to the present, though what I saw made me believe I was dreaming. A silver BMW rolled to a stop, and as I slowly walked down the stairs, still disbelieving my eyes, Danny Gorman got out of the driver's door. I ran down the walk, smiling in welcome. No, I didn't love him, but at least he had come, and a friend right now was a godsend.

The other door opened and all five-feet-one of Susie North appeared. Two friends!

I hugged them both. "Why didn't you tell me you were coming?" I asked as I hugged them again. "It's so good to see you guys. Boy, it's been some week, I'll tell you that! What brought you guys all the way up here?"

Danny looked down at the grass, and Susie said, "Ellen, I know this isn't the right way to tell you this, but darned if I can figure out a better way. Go ahead, Dan, tell her.''

Grandmother called me from the porch. ''Ellen?''

I tugged on their hands. ''Tell me in a minute. I want you to meet my grandmother and her friend.''

''But, Ellen—'' Danny protested.

I ignored him. ''Come on.''

They followed me into the house, and I was so pleased to see them, let alone the sight of Gerald and Grandmother standing next to each other as if they'd done it for a lifetime, that I completely forgot exactly who Grandma thought Danny was.

''This is Susie North and this is Danny Gorman,'' I said.

It hit me as Grandmother's face erupted into a huge smile. ''Your fiancé! Danny, welcome, dear.''

He was given a one-armed hug by my grandmother. I tried to use sign language to tell him just to go along with it, but Susie blurted out, ''Her fiancé? No, no, Mrs. Brookfield. Danny is my husband!'' She innocently trotted out her left hand, which was suitably decorated with a sparkling diamond ring and a gold band, and added, ''We just got married day before yesterday!''

You could have heard the proverbial pin drop. Gerald looked as if he wanted to disappear, Grandmother's eyes narrowed, I took Danny and Susie by the hands and pulled them back outside to their car. ''It's been great to see you," I said. "And congratulations on your marriage."

"Then you're not angry or hurt?" Danny asked.

I kissed him on the cheek. "Heavens no. Silly boy. Live long and prosper, and all that. I'll be in touch. Have a nice honeymoon."

So they drove off, and my last image of them was Susie looking out her window, her face puzzled.

Well, who could blame her?

Grandmother was beside herself. It was as though the past was being revisited, and on the heels of her reconciliation with Gerald, it was just about too much. I figured (like the chicken I was) that the less I said, the better. I got her into bed again, brewed a pot of tea, put together a quick dinner, and served it to her in bed. Gerald sat glued to her side like a limpet to a rock.

"Ellen, Ellen," she lamented. "To have this happen to you—oh dear, I know how you must feel."

"I feel fine," I assured her. I gave her a pill and stood by till she took it. Her face was too pale again.

"But after I did what I did—oh, you shouldn't even speak to me!" She looked at Gerald and added, "I really didn't faint, Gerry. I just didn't want Ellen to leave. I'm despicable, aren't I?"

"Totally," he said.

I just looked at her, too stunned for a moment to speak. When my voice did return I took a step closer and said, "You tricked me into staying? How dare you!"

"Mimi, is that all you did?" Gerald asked.

"Is that all she did? I've been walking around on egg shells, afraid I'd say or do the wrong thing—"

She apparently decided Gerald was fonder of her at the moment than I was going to be for quite a while, and she interrupted me to direct her next comment to him. "I didn't know that her fiancé was going to abandon her, did I? I was acting in her best interest."

"What else did you do, Mimi?" Gerald asked gently.

"I told Josh—well, never mind what I told him."

Gerald and I exchanged long looks. Then he said, "The skiff is tied up to the dock. Take your time."

"And you take care of her," I said as I ran for the door.

"I plan to," he answered firmly.

Chapter Thirteen

I'll be angry at her later, I told myself as I ran toward the bay. Sure enough, the skiff was tied up to the dock. Breathless from the long run, I hopped inside, untied the ropes, and promptly began drifting south.

How in the world did one go about starting an outboard engine?

I floated under the nearby dock, the bow nudging against the rocky shoreline while the rotting pilings towered over my head. A dozen rats were looking at me—I just knew it—but I would have happily taken them all home for a week if I could just figure out how to start the engine.

"Use your head!" I shouted.

I used an oar first to get the boat turned in the right direction. Then I pulled the black cord on the top of the outboard. Other than my shoulder being dislocated, not much happened. I pulled the cord again and again, and finally it caught and the engine sputtered. I'd never heard a more beautiful sound!

Eventually, I figured out how to get it into forward gear, and I began my fitful trip across the bay. There were three boats tied up to Oyster Island: the larger motorboat, the small sailboat, and Mr. Brennan's larger sailboat. There was a light on inside Mr. Brennan's boat.

As I plowed into the float, Quincy hurled himself into the skiff, which pushed me away from the float and into the side of the larger sailboat. I heard a crunch, and when I pushed away, I saw that I'd left a five-inch gash in the newly painted wood.

What a great way to impress someone.

Josh's head appeared in the main hatch.

"What the—" He stopped when he saw it was me. "Ellen?"

"Blame your dog," I said as Quincy abandoned the skiff in favor of the sailboat. I was holding on to the side of the sailboat to keep from drifting off. I wasn't quite sure how to get the boat over to the dock without letting go, and I wasn't letting go, because the engine had died and I didn't know if I could get it started again.

Josh climbed out into the cockpit and then leaned down over the side of the sailboat. He held on to the skiff and said, "Now, you hand me a rope, okay?"

So I scampered into the bow and got the rope and handed it to Josh, who got off the sailboat and hauled me back to the clear spot on the float. He tied the boat, then put a hand out.

"Are you getting out?" he asked.

"I don't know," I said. "Do you want me to?"

He sat down on the float, his feet in the skiff. He was wearing tan pants and a blue shirt, and he hadn't shaved in a day or two. He looked perfect: handsome enough to twist my heart, and yet just a little disheveled, a fact I took to mean that without me, he just wasn't up to par.

"Your grandmother said that I was confusing you. She said that you were engaged to some guy down south and that any day, he was coming north to marry you and that if I cared for you, I should leave you alone and let you marry the man you loved. She pointed out that a woman alone for the summer with just a cranky old woman for company was bound to be attracted to a handsome fellow like me, and I quote that last part. She also said that we were all involved in a highly emotionally charged situation, one that was bound to confuse a person."

"Were you confused?" I asked.

He shook his head slowly. "No, I wasn't confused."

"What weren't you confused about?"

"I knew I loved you, Ellen. But part of what she said made sense. I agreed to give you some space and to make it look as though it was my idea."

"Didn't I tell you once, I believe it was at the beach, not to be a quitter? How could you have doubted how I felt about you?"

He laughed. "If I remember the scene correctly, Ellen, my love, you also told me you had told your grandmother you were engaged. I believe you said the whole thing was very complicated."

"If you're going to go holding a person to every silly thing that passes through her lips. . . ."

He smiled. He took my hand and pulled me up to sit beside him on the float. The water slapped against the wood as he said, "I was afraid. I was afraid that I loved you and you didn't love me, at least not the same way."

"I was afraid of the same thing," I admitted.

Josh took my hand in both of his, raised it to his lips and kissed my fingers. "It felt as though I died this week. It felt as though life had drained of color and sound and smell. My grandfather got more cheerful by the day, while I felt as if I was sinking into quick-sand."

"I know." I smoothed his dark hair away from his face. His eyes were darker than the water, compelling. "I felt the same way."

"Do you know how the marching band went today?"

"They're together right now," I said. "He's calling her Mimi and she's calling him Gerry. I suspect they've even kissed a few times, just for old times' sake."

"Which is what we should be doing." Josh drew me closer till his unshaved chin touched my forehead. Then his lips found mine, and he kissed me once, softly, as though to reestablish who and what we were to each other. He drew away from me and cupped my face in his hands, and he whispered, "I love you, Ellen."

"I love you too," I said.

"You're not moving back to Oakland, are you?" he asked softly as his lips brushed my eyelids, my cheek, my throat.

"Is that an invitation?" I asked.

"That's an invitation," he said softly. "One of those lifetime kind. The kind the new generation of Holt men don't go back on."

"Then I'm not going back to Oakland." I raised his chin until our eyes met, and then we sealed the deal with a kiss.

...great Early
... d David Hume. ...
...ysics and mathematics
...d from which modern science
...developed; and Hume's philo-
...eas and arguments are the proximate
... a significant part of modern critical and
...alytical philosophy. Thus the works of Newton
and Hume have been of profound and increasing
interest to philosophers and historians in recent
years."

Did Hume, in his attack on the argument from
design, have Newton's scientific theism in mind,
as well as pre-Newtonian versions of the design
argument? The author establishes conclusively
that he did. Beyond that, he examines the co-
gency of Hume's attack and shows that it was,
and remains, devastating to the argument from
design.

Mr. Hurlbutt's purpose—to convey an under-
standing of scientific theism in terms of its
nature, its sources or origins, and its fate and
validity—is reflected in the organization of the
book. In Part One, "Newtonianism," he describes
and analyzes the ways in which Newton and his
contemporaries reformulated the classical design
argument in terms of the new physics and optics.
The author also compares and contrasts Newton's scientific theism with other current theo-
logical views, among them those of Bacon, the
Cambridge Platonists, Boyle, Locke, the Deists,
Berkeley, and Butler. Part Two, "The Ancient
and Medieval Context of the Design Argument,"
inquires into the classical origins of Newtonian
theism and traces the design argument, along
with its attendant logical formula, argument by
analogy, from Plato to Galileo. In Part Three,
"The Denouement: Hume and the Design Argument," Mr. Hurlbutt sets out to prove the thesis